DON'T

RUN

DON'T

RUN

A NOVEL
BY

SUSAN J. CROCKFORD

For my friend Val Geist and his
neighbours in the Alberni Valley,
who fended off attacking wolves

Acknowledgements

This book is a work of science-based fiction. With two exceptions, all names are fictitious and any resemblance to characters living or dead is entirely coincidental.

I assigned real names to a pair of fictitious characters as reward for the winners of a reader-support contest held several years ago. The financial assistance provided by my fantastic supporters made it possible for me to publish my serious science volume, *Polar Bear Evolution*, and for that I will be eternally grateful. Congratulations John Macgowan and Ned Komar, you are the winners!

I should note that "RCMP" refers to the Royal Canadian Mounted Police (we call them Mounties), who are responsible for policing and emergency response in all rural and many suburban areas of Canada. While Mounties could not have been left out of a story such as this, I may have imagined them to behave in ways that are contrary to current policy.

The same is true for the various First Nations and their members who inhabit lands in and around the town of Tofino—they could not have been left out. I have spent my entire career as an archaeozoologist working with respected First Nations individuals from the west coast of Vancouver Island and I've learned a lot from this long association. However, this book is a novel and the characters and specific dialogue portrayed in response to the imaginary future crisis I've envisioned are entirely fictitious.

The people who assisted in envisioning and preparing this story for publication will for now remain anonymous but I thank them with all my heart. You know who you are, except for my good friend Val Geist, who unfortunately did not live to see the idea come to fruition.

Prologue

It's the winter of 2028/2029.

Four years have passed since Newfoundland suffered unprecedented fatal attacks by hungry polar bears. However, on the opposite side of Canada, the little surfing town of Tofino has a big problem with wolves it never saw coming.

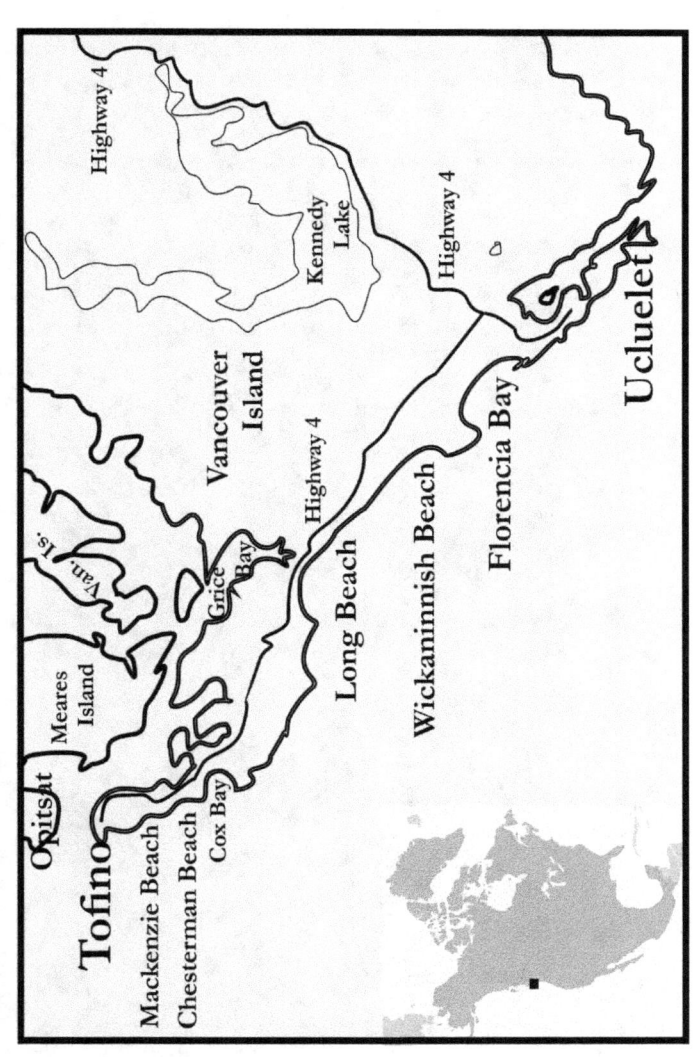

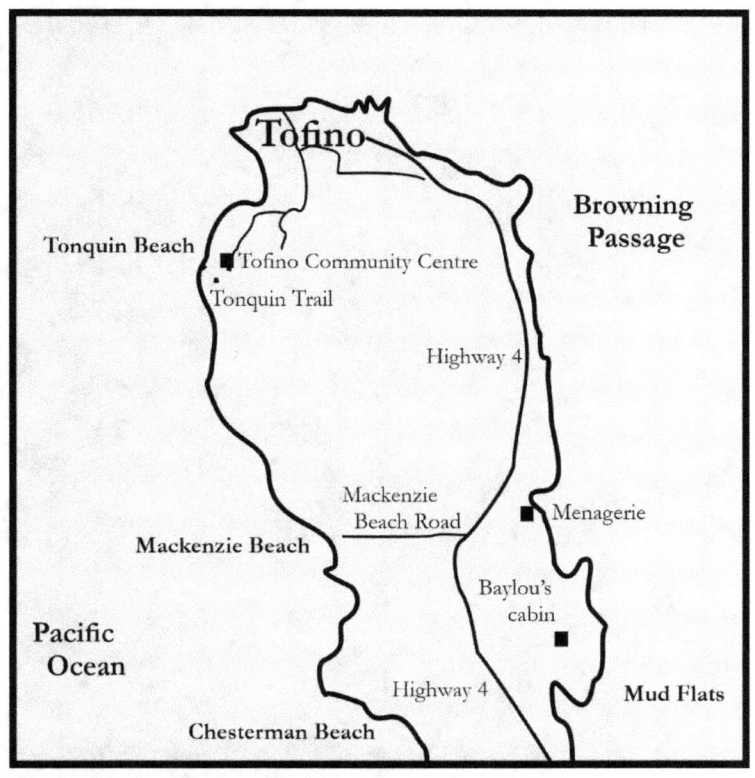

Some Tofino area locations mentioned in the story.

Chapter 1

Sunday 10 December 10:15 a.m.

Baylou awoke after sunrise, having slept in after her long bike ride the day before. Her tiny cabin showed its age. It had been built sometime in the 1960s and was still standing only because hastily-applied rough timber boards had been nailed into place at various stress points. Isolated bits of the original cedar shake roof were silvered with age, pops of brightness against the newer burnt-orange patches now bound together by thick mats of rain-forest moss.

She pulled on the worn, dirty jeans and thick flannel shirt she wore most days and brewed a cup of tea made from dried rosehips gathered from her garden. She gently pulled open the door, its ancient hinges squealing in useless complaint. Slipping her feet into stiff work boots lying to the left of the door, she pulled on a massive sheepskin jacket as she cleared the threshold. The floor boards of the sagging porch groaned as she took a step outside.

Junior was not on the old wool blanket she'd folded up for him under the window. The big black dog had again refused to come in last night and she hadn't forced him, knowing his protective streak couldn't be reasoned with.

She walked over to the worn front steps and brushed several inches of new snow off the one that was second-from-the-top. It was her preferred porch seating spot since she kept the only chair she owned inside. She whistled and called several times but Junior didn't burst out from behind the huge covered wood pile or sprint down the path from the garden as she expected. Her pale eyebrows wrinkled in a frown as she scanned the dark trees that ringed the property, their branches still laden with snow from last night's storm.

Abruptly, she slammed her mug of tea down on the tree stump next to the stairs that served as a makeshift side table, splashing some of the liquid high in the air.

In a fluid movement that belied her age, she bent over and tied her boots, then reached back onto the porch to grab the stout stick with the duck-shaped knot at one end that she carried when she walked the property.

Calling for Junior again as she went, she descended the steps and took long strides along the snow-covered path that led towards the garden and roughly-built chicken coop.

Baylou saw a black form lying in the snow near the far edge of her carefully tilled grounds. She hesitated momentarily and then, walking faster, she stopped short at the end of the berry patch and looked down.

A low moan of anguish escaped her lips as she lowered herself to the ground beside his ruined body. There was blood everywhere. Both his throat and stomach had been ripped open.

His once magnificent, shaggy head was as it had been last night, unharmed except for the dull, lifeless eyes. She pulled it onto her lap and stroked the long, wavy black fur and fondled the velvety ears.

"Stupid, lousy watch dog," she whispered tenderly. Tears welled up in her eyes as she murmured his name, until great streams of brine ran down her face.

After a few minutes, she brushed the wet away with her sleeve and glanced over at the chicken coop. Suddenly her head spun around towards the forest. She stared for several minutes in that direction, scanning the edge of the dark woods, but eventually looked back at the chickens, which were raising a ruckus as if only now something had happened worth announcing.

Aided by the stick, Baylou eased herself up from the damp ground and brushed herself off. As she looked over the body again, she took two steps forward, looking down at some undisturbed snow near Junior's tail. She couldn't have missed the significance of the two big paw prints.

All the recent howling she'd heard made sense now. She knew who had done this.

"Bastard," she said, in a low voice fierce enough to make the chickens squawk.

***

Baylou was older than her cabin and equally scruffy. Broad-shouldered and an inch over six feet tall, her once-legendary physical strength had waned in the last two decades and her teeth were in bad shape. Decades of isolation had taken a toll on her mental health, exacerbating her natural anti-social tendencies. The long mane of blonde curls that had once made her stand out amongst the hippie crowd on the beach had been hacked off to shoulder length and was now so heavily streaked with silver it was almost white. The azure eyes of her youth had similarly paled to a cloudy ice blue.

She'd come to the west coast of Vancouver Island the summer of 1969. In those days, you could drive your car out onto the spectacular majesty of Long Beach and not stop until you'd put almost 10 miles of sand behind you. Only 19 years old then, she'd joined dozens of others who lived year-round in tents and makeshift log shelters a bit further south at Florencia Bay. That all changed in '71 when the Canadian federal government wrestled control over the expanse of forest and sand wedged between Tofino and Ucluelet, and made everything about fees and rules. Camping and driving on the beach were among the first things to go.

She'd moved north then, from the beach to the nearby town of Tofino, as if it hadn't occurred to her to go elsewhere—or simply go home, as some of the squatters had done. In that first decade or so, the struggle for

4

survival became second nature to her. She'd always had trouble finding housing, which came down to the fact she seldom had more than a few dollars to her name. Tenting and couch-surfing through the '70s and most of the '80s, she'd resorted to renting something over the winter only if she'd been able to put some funds aside from the odd bit of summer work.

When Michael Poole set up his 10-acre commune off Mackenzie Beach Road in '88, she'd been one of the first to move in. Her hippie neighbours were much more politically-minded than she'd ever been but their exuberant passions often carried her along like a house seized by floodwaters.

Tensions around clearcut logging had been strong among the residents of Poole's Land and in '93 they erupted into high-profile protests attended by thousands of others from outside the community. 'War in the Woods', they'd called it.

Everything had changed for her then. By the time things settled down, she'd come to own this dilapidated cabin nestled deep in the forest just south of town.

Chapter 2

Sunday 10 December 5:15 p.m.

Luke pulled into the grocery store parking lot, intending to pick up chips and cheese to make nachos for dinner, a meal he could rustle up quickly in the up-scale motel's toaster oven. As he cruised through the aisles, the meal he envisioned became more and more grandiose. Adding a jar of olives, a stick of pepperoni, and some spicy salsa to his basket, he went in search of garlic, lime, and avocados for a guacamole that now seemed essential.

Scanning the mass of avocados, he searched in vain for two that were fit for immediate consumption. Cursing under his breath but perhaps louder than he had intended, he was startled by a comment from someone standing next to him.

"You're planning well ahead for your nacho dinner next week, I see. Smart thinking. Expecting to buy a ripe avocado on the day you plan to eat it is a fool's errand only a novice would entertain."

Luke's head swivelled hard right and his mouth gapped in surprise. Beside him stood a brown-haired, grey-eyed woman about six inches shorter than his 6'4" frame and about his age, with a face almost as familiar to him as the one that greeted him in the mirror every morning. It was, however, one he hadn't seen in at least a decade.

"Blake? What the hell?"

"Well, well! I've heard the produce section suggested as a place to meet an eligible bachelor, not a long-lost friend."

The two stood staring at each other for a few seconds until Luke leaned over and pulled her in for a bear hug of epic proportions.

"It's good to see you, Luke," said Blake, her voice muffled against his shoulder. "It's been too long. What the hell are you doing here?"

"Just visiting," replied Luke, easing himself back to take a better look at his friend. "And you?"

"I work here. I thought you'd have heard. I got transferred to the Tofino detachment three years ago. Just before I heard about your trouble with the bears in Newfoundland. I tried to get in touch when I heard the news but I guess my message never made it through. Then I got caught up in the stress of starting a new post and just forgot to follow up."

"Yeah, it was a crazy time," Luke said. "Chaotic would be putting it mildly."

"How long are you staying?"

"Until the end of the month, I think. An extended vacation of sorts."

"Come for dinner then. Unless your failed meal plan involved someone else?"

"No, just me," Luke explained. "You've got something else in mind that beats nachos without guacamole?"

"Let's grab some steaks," she replied. "I don't live far."

"Perfect," said Luke, still looking a bit stunned. "I just came from stocking up on beer, thinking to buy enough for my entire stay. There should be enough in my truck to get us through dinner."

"Dream on, my friend," blustered Blake. "Don't worry, though, I've got whiskey."

***

While they shopped, they resumed a long-standing debate regarding the relative virtues of potatoes and garlic bread when paired with steak, and whether T-bone or ribeye was the best cut. They settled on bread, since garlicked loaves pre-wrapped in foil sat conveniently above the steak section, and ribeye, since T-bones weren't even on offer.

As they walked out to the parking lot with their groceries, Blake pointed to a newer-model red Ford 350 crew-cab parked at the far end of the lot.

Luke smiled, remembering Blake's penchant for powerful vehicles.

"Just follow me out," she said "My place is off the Mackenzie Beach Road."

Luke found his own truck and maneuvered it into position behind Blake's at the parking lot exit. They pulled out in tandem and he followed her south along the road out of town, turning right towards Mackenzie Beach behind her, and then right again when she headed up a short, snow-dusted track into the woods.

"How long has it been—ten years?" asked Luke, as Blake handed him one of his recently-purchased beers as she transferred a dozen of them into the fridge. She settled in across from him at the booth-style table as he took a long, satisfying pull from the bottle.

"Thirteen," she replied without hesitation. "Last time I saw you was at the funeral in Yellowknife for those two sergeants that got caught in the storm. Remember? I think that was the last time the four of us from the academy that went north on graduation were all together."

"Seems hard to believe it's been that long."

There were a few moments of silence as both of them drank, gazing not at each other but at the reflections in the window, seemingly deep in thought.

Luke had known Blake Josephine Palmer since their university days. They had run into each other at a local pub in first year when the set of friends each had arrived with had merged into one big table and they found themselves sitting next to each other.

As they'd chatted, they'd discovered that they had grown up in similar small towns in Alberta. Blake had opened up about herself in such an easy and natural way that he'd willingly done the same. After an hour, he felt they had been friends forever.

Both had been adventurous, out-going kids from reserved, anti-intellectual hunting families. Luke was an older brother by 10 years to a sister he'd been devoted to, while Blake had a much older, protective brother she adored. Both had expressed a strong desire for a different kind of future than the ones their families were advocating.

Blake had enrolled in sociology, thinking it suited her personality. Luke had headed into wildlife management, rashly assuming it would fit his love of animals. Neither choice had generated parental approval, but that hadn't bothered them. Ultimately, both of them had been miserable with their choices but they'd persevered to the end, mostly to avoid giving their parents the satisfaction of being right.

However, neither of them had given even a passing thought to pursuing a career in their respective fields of study but couldn't think of what else to do. Then, in their final year, Luke discovered the RCMP would consider potential police recruits with any sort of degree. Luke and Blake both applied and were accepted, although Blake only barely passed the strenuous fitness exam. Both sets of parents again weren't thrilled but didn't actually disapprove, so off they went to become Mounties.

Although Blake was very proud of her accomplishment, even she had to admit that Luke's tall, muscular physique filled out the red serge dress uniform infinitely better than hers did—and that his almost-black hair and deep brown eyes really complemented the traditional colour scheme.

During those years at university and the police academy, they'd had an on-again-off-again sexual relationship that sooner or later would revert to friendship. Romance between them never seemed to stick.

They were compatible in so many ways it always came as a shock to them both to find they couldn't sustain intense physical and emotional intimacy for more than a few months. It left them raw every time and the last go-around had been the worst.

Blake had been aloof but cordial to him when they'd run into each other in Yellowknife a few months after their last split and Luke had convinced himself he'd never hear from her again. These last few years, he'd often missed the comfort of her friendship but each time he'd thought of reaching out, his fear of being rebuffed had changed his mind.

Just as he wondered why she hadn't walked right past him in the grocery store this afternoon, he knew the answer and wondered why he hadn't thought of it before. He always known she didn't hold a grudge for long, especially with him. Something else had been making him reluctant to resume their friendship. Perhaps a need to leave open the possibility of something a whole lot easier and less volatile if it was given some breathing room? Maybe hoping—beyond reason, actually—for something like what he'd eventually had with Kate?

The quiet meow of an enormous, long-haired black cat with bright amber eyes shattered the stillness of the moment as it sauntered into the room and parked itself in front of Luke. It looked up at him and meowed again.

"That's Cooper," said Blake, laughing out loud. "An abandoned pet that was living in the forest until he adopted me. He'll demand food from anyone."

She jumped up and stepped into the small kitchen behind her. Grabbing a tin of cat food from one of the cupboards, she opened the pop-top and plopped the loose contents into a bowl on the floor, which Luke now noticed peaking around the corner of the fridge.

"That should keep him quiet for a while," she said, sitting back down. "He'll happily eat kibble if no one's here but to him, people mean wet food."

"That's a big cat," said Luke, stating the obvious.

"Yeah, he really grew into himself. He was a really scrawny kitten when he first started hanging around and I took pity on him. Now he's heavier than he looks and strong as a bobcat."

She turned away from the cat and leveled her eyes at him.

"So, what brought you here?" she asked pointedly, redirecting the conversation.

He shrugged.

"I had to get out. I'm on unpaid leave 'til next August. I kind of headed west from Newfoundland until I ran out of road."

"Frankly, it hasn't been a picnic for me but I wouldn't have pegged you for being unhappy on the job," she said

12

more bluntly than she intended. "Did the polar bear crisis really do you in that badly?"

"It was more complicated than that, but yeah. I'm going to give photography a go, see if I can make it work as a business."

Blake got to her feet, breaking the slightly awkward moment.

"Let's put the steaks on, grill should be hot enough by now," she said, grabbing the steaks and foil-wrapped bread from the counter as she headed for the door.

Luke followed her out, looking around again at the spacious interior. He'd never been in such a large trailer before. It seemed almost as large as some of the permanently-installed prefabricated homes he'd seen that were 'mobile' in name only.

It wasn't the kind of motor home with the built-in engine that he'd noticed on his way west, the ones that struggled to get over the mountain passes. It was a 5th wheel trailer with several pop-outs on the sides, meant to be towed by a big pickup truck like the one Blake drove.

The trailer was now supported by a concrete pillar at the hitch end, with an enormous timber deck built off one side covered by a retractable canvas awning. Clearly Blake didn't intend to move it any time soon, which freed up her truck for everyday getting around.

There seemed to be everything a single person could need. Blake had shown him around when they'd first come in, pointing out a pull-down outdoor cooking set-up as she'd turned on the grill to pre-heat for the steaks.

Inside, there was a queen-sized bed up front, a full-sized bathroom with shower, a stacked washer and dryer, and a fully-equipped kitchen with booth-style table and benches for eating or writing. At the tail end, there was a pair of recliner chairs opposite a bookcase flanking a TV screen and gas fireplace.

"Medium-rare still suit you?" asked Blake, brushing off a layer of snow and plopping the bread down on the grill beside the two slabs of meat.

"Of course," Luke huffed, feigning offense at the suggestion that his meat preferences might have changed over time.

Blake had flipped on a set of outdoor lights that made the snow in the nearby trees sparkle. Luke asked about the unusual setup, and she pointed out the power and septic tank hook-ups, as well as the locked garbage shed off to one side.

"When I got to Tofino, there was already another female corporal at the detachment who I was forced to bunk with. We just didn't get on but there was really no other option. There was only the one double room and two women: no singles were available. I don't know why men think women should automatically get along. She was a real piece of work, that one. I don't understand how she ever qualified. Not just opinionated but demanded I get on board her latest illogical tropes. She just never shut up.

"Anyway, one day I reached my limit. I told the Sergeant I wasn't prepared to file a harassment complaint against her but that if he didn't let me find alternative quarters, I'd quit outright."

"Wow," Luke responded. "You're lucky you didn't get canned just for that."

"Yeah, I know," Blake said with a grin. "But there'd already been trouble keeping staff out here, so he was in a bind. He agreed I could move out as long as I could find something within a 5-minute siren ride of downtown. I kept asking around and eventually found the guy who owns this land, John Macgowan.

"He has a few local investment properties around town and when he found out I was a Mountie, he agreed to rent it to me for a very reasonable price if I could find a trailer of some kind to put on it. I didn't even have to explain about not being able to afford tourist prices—turned out Mounties were his soft spot."

"Next day off, I went to Nanaimo and bought this beauty," she said, arms spread towards the trailer. "It was actually cheaper than my truck, if you can believe it. But you know me, I never really spend money except on my vehicles, so I had enough in the bank. The septic, water, and power were already in place, I just needed to get hooked up."

The sound of sputtering of fat made her break away to flip the steaks and rotate the bread. Turning away from the grill, her focus shifted back to him.

"When did you say you got here? Last week?"

"First of December, week ago Wednesday."

"And where are you staying?"

"It was tough going but I eventually found a motel with a last-minute cancellation on a month-long reservation just out of town. I had no idea Tofino would be such a popular place at this time of year.

"And I know it's only been a week but I've been exploring and taking pictures around town. I've been approached several times to take photos at some particular spot and one couple insisted on buying me a beer in return for the image I took. I realized that maybe I have a knack for capturing the essence of the special memories these people seem to be after. And it makes me think that ability just might be desirable enough to be the foundation of a profitable business."

"Sounds promising," said Blake, piling the steaks on a plate and crowning them with the hot bread log. "But let's take these babies inside, I think we're done here."

After a hasty distribution of plates, utensils, and fresh bottles of beer, they settled in to eat. Between bites, Blake regaled Luke some stories of her first year in Tofino.

When they were done, she moved the dregs of the meal to the counter and grabbed them each another beer from the fridge.

"So, explain to me the complicated part about why you're here," Blake demanded in a soft encouraging tone. "From the beginning."

Chapter 3

Sunday 10 December 8:35 pm

"Well, I'd transferred to St. John's after my five-year stint in Resolute, which I think you already know," Luke replied, looking out the window into the darkness. "I had a girl up north, named Rosie. We'd gotten really close but it turned out she loved Resolute more than me, so I went to Newfoundland alone.

"I met Kate when the polar bear situation blew up that spring. She'd recently lost her husband during a grizzly attack. We had a bit of a rocky start, in that she wasn't quite ready for a new relationship. But we got closer once things settled down. Before long, we realized we were solidly in love.

"By then, I'd transferred permanently to the detachment at Fogo Island, where she lived, after the sergeant in charge decided to retire. There were still problems with bears along the north coast and a strong likelihood there would continue to be ongoing issues for at least a few more years. The boss in St. John's agreed that my expertise would continue to come in handy and that I could just as easily serve the region from Fogo as well as from the city. Overall, it seemed like the right time and place to settle down and she agreed to marry me, with a wedding planned for the next summer.

"Then the ice tsunami hit in March. You must have heard about that?" he asked, his voice dropping as he glanced over at her.

Blake just nodded.

"Kate and her dog had gone over to visit a friend on Cape Breton in Nova Scotia. They were staying at a beach-front cottage in Sydney when the waves hit. They were just in the wrong place at the wrong time. The ice wiped out everything in that area of the coast.

"But she wasn't supposed to be there, she was meant to be in another house south of town. So, when she didn't call after the crisis was over, I was frantic to find her. I arranged to be deployed to help with the cleanup but it was pointless. Kate, the dog, her friend, the whole neighbourhood, they were all gone."

"I never found her," he said under his breath, his voice finally breaking.

Blake reached over and laid her hand on his arm. He looked back out the window, at the nothingness.

"It was all too much, after all that went on during the bear attacks the year before. Too much grief. By the fall, I realized I wasn't really functioning and took six months leave—then another, and another. I figured a year and a half was plenty of time to heal.

"I bought myself a wide-angle lens to complement the two telephotos I already owned and spent my time exploring Newfoundland, obsessively taking photos I never showed to anyone. It felt like I was getting better.

"Then spring this year brought heavy ice from the north again and with it a boat load of more polar bear problems. No fatal attacks on people, thankfully, but a half dozen or so very close calls. And every report of those, even though I didn't have to deal with them all myself, made me think of Kate."

"It broke my heart all over again," he almost whispered.

"By the end of the summer, I realized I simply had to go. Newfoundland just wasn't the place for me anymore. I needed a new start. I'd wanted to quit outright but the boss talked me into taking a year without pay. I really doubted a year would make any difference but I agreed. Quite honestly, I was too tired to argue.

"So, I packed a few things and started driving. As I made my way across the country, I continued to take pictures, and an idea grew at the back of my mind to develop a photography business.

"I'd been an RCMP wildlife safety officer for more than twenty years. I needed to be something else. I was only 46, young enough to start again. I realized that if I worked for a bit after the year of leave was up and then retired, I'd be eligible for a full pension. I had savings I could live on until then but figured some cash income would mean I'd draw the pot down less quickly.

"By the time I'd reached western Ontario, it really started to feel like a new beginning," he said in a lighter tone, finally taking a swig of his beer. Blake did the same but realized her bottle was empty.

She got up to fetch another from the fridge.

"When was that?" she encouraged, taking a sip.

"Middle of October or so. I'd been taking my time. I poked around the back roads and wilderness parks. I tried to focus on the less obvious beauty, especially the little critters. The local birds and other animals that are always around, that people seldom notice. I practiced playing with light and exposure, teaching myself to see things a little differently, learning to find just the right light, the right angle. It's amazing how much difference those things make."

"But how did you end up here?" Blake asked.

"I just kept driving. I'd never seen the Pacific Ocean. For some reason, I sort of thought that Vancouver was the end of the road but then I discovered there was a ferry over to Vancouver Island, so I kept going until I got here."

"And what did you think of the drive across the island?" Blake asked with a knowing smile.

"Mountains everywhere! Not Rocky Mountain-sized but still! If I wasn't on one, they were in the background or staring me in the face. Once I hit the rain forest, I was smitten, even though I needed my rain gear almost every day. It's so different from Newfoundland, I suddenly felt I was in just the right place."

"And Tofino?"

"How did I not know that people come here just to walk on the beach in the middle of a storm?" he asked, incredulously. "When did incessant rain become a tourist attraction?"

Blake shook her head and shrugged.

"Well, as you've seen this week, even in winter we get the odd few hours of sunshine between storms," she added. "And when it clears up just before sunset, it can be quite glorious. We get visitors from all over the world and as busy as it is now, summer is ten times worse. It's crazy."

"Yeah, we should be at the slowest part of the slow season but there are still lots of people around," Luke replied. "A guy at the surf shop said the water is cold all the time but a wet suit makes it tolerable. And that some of the biggest storms and wildest waves come during the winter, which seems to be what a lot of folks are after, whether they're here to surf or not."

"And there's so much great scenery," he added. "My guess is I've only seen the most obvious of them: long sandy beaches with gorgeous sunsets, deep moody forests, and cliff tops with spectacular views, all within 20 miles of town. It's made me think I could focus on special event photography—like, for the brides I'm told insist on wading into the surf in their wedding gowns."

Blake scoffed, shaking her head in disapproval. After draining her beer, she spoke in a more muted tone.

"Does that mean you're going to stay? As in, quit the force and live here as a civilian? I'm fast getting fed up with the job myself, but I never thought I see that happening to you."

Luke looked into her hazel eyes and his facial expression softened.

"Yeah, I think so. I can't imagine going back, which I think means I'm about done with policing. And at least for now, photography is what I need to do. What I have in mind is a long way from the wildlife photography I'd started out envisioning but it feels like the right focus and the right place. Feels even more right knowing you're here too."

"Where are you going to stay?" Blake asked, trying to sound nonchalant.

"I have no idea. It was hard enough trying to find a short-term rental—I expect affordable permanent housing is even more scarce. I haven't even started looking, but I've got the motel 'til the end of the month so I'm not in a panic quite yet."

Blake got up and grabbed a bottle of rye whiskey and two short glasses from one of the cupboards and set them on the table. As she poured out the liquor, she looked over at him.

"Why don't I give my landlord John a call about a local rental? He might have a house or basement suite available somewhere."

"That would be great, Blake, thanks."

"Until then, why don't you stop in at the detachment office and introduce yourself? You might as well. You know they'll find out eventually. Better not to piss them off if you're going to hang around. You know how they are."

"True enough. I'll do that next week."

And then the real drinking and talking began as they caught each other up on family news and insider stories of the police business they'd both been involved in since they'd last really spoken. Blake pleaded with Luke to reveal the unpublished details about the Newfoundland polar bear attacks that had so dominated the newspapers a few years ago. As he obliged, he found it oddly cathartic to tell her everything that had happened.

***

Hours later, Blake pulled out the extra bed in the living room for him, since he was clearly in no condition to drive back to the motel.

As she turned to head off to her bedroom, he'd caught her arm and swung her back to face him.

"Good night," he whispered, taking her face in his hands. He kissed her gently and sighed with relief when she kissed him back with some enthusiasm.

There was forgiveness in her response but not the yearning that in the past had gotten them into trouble. There was no implied invitation for him to follow as she'd broken away and headed down the hall, which left him both grateful and a bit disappointed.

After a few hours of sleep, he discretely let himself out the door as the cat gave him a surly glance from the kitchen.

Chapter 4

Tuesday 12 December 9:55 am

After spending Monday recovering from his reunion with Blake, he set out after breakfast to visit the office of the local RCMP, which was right downtown.

The officers at the detachment, including Blake's boss, seemed like a good bunch but none of them had been there for long. Even the Sergeant had only been there for three years. None of them had had much experience with animal trouble either, which was often the case in small towns like this one.

"Dealing with nuisance wildlife has been my on-the-job specialty," he told Sergeant Bob Hammond. "Since I'm very familiar with the havoc predators can cause, especially bears, I generally get assigned to districts with the biggest potential or active problems. Right now, I'm on extended medical leave from the force, so I'm not here in any professional capacity."

The look on Hammond's face when he said that seemed oddly relieved, but he shook off the feeling and asked about the sergeant's time here.

He got an earful.

"You should know that a lot has changed since I got here," Hammond said, taking a deep breath. "I have to remind myself I was part of that change, since it does seem that things kind of fell apart soon after I arrived.

"As you know, it wasn't just here—things were changing everywhere. What they tell me is that for more than a decade before I arrived, Tofino had been as solidly far-left politically as you could get and seemed unlikely to shift. But because it's such a small, unique community, those outside changes were eventually strong enough to have an impact."

"What do you mean by that?" asked Luke, genuinely curious.

"For one thing, a lot of folks who'd been here since the early 2000s suddenly up and moved out, including the town veterinarian and many of our critical care doctors and nurses. The Sergeant who I replaced had been here almost 10 years. Some well-connected people died suddenly and a number of influential businesses and non-profits went belly-up. Local First Nations lost their bid to control access to public trails and beaches. New folks moved in and the political tenor of the place shifted.

"That famous former politician we're not supposed to talk about left as well—you know the one I mean, the surfer my father's generation called Skippy. Essentially driven out of town by negative attention."

"I hadn't heard about that," said Luke. "I'd have thought he was immune to that kind of pressure."

"Yeah, I think his ego simply couldn't take it anymore," Hammond replied. "Soon after, town council made some amendments to business regulations to try and stimulate new growth. But the outfits that moved in caused friction with the old guard. Folks are trying to make it all work but it's a struggle at times."

"I've seen contentious issues play out in small towns before," Luke commented with a shake of his head. "It can really get ugly."

"Well, on the whole it hasn't been that bad, at least not yet," replied Hammond. "But we used to have a non-profit group that dealt informally with wildlife issues around town. Its leader, who I never got a chance to meet, died suddenly just days after I arrived. A power struggle erupted between several of the volunteers he worked with, about who should take over. The in-fighting blew up the group and it still hasn't recovered. I'm told the group made a real, one-on-one effort to educate tourists, which helped by preventing trouble before it started, especially with bears."

"I've seen some of those organizations at work myself," Luke replied. "They can really make a difference, especially with tourists who aren't used to living with big predators on a day-to-day basis."

Bob turned and picked up a colourful pamphlet from the counter behind him, which he handed to Luke.

"This information is all we've got at the moment, which Parks Canada people hand out to visitors and distributes around town."

"Slick," commented Luke, flipping it open for a quick look. "I think I've seen some of these on the ground at parking lots in the Park and around town."

"Yeah, well, that's the problem. I doubt if many people even open the things up, they just toss them aside. I really hope this local group manage to pull something together for this summer because the detachment's been fielding way too many nuisance calls about wildlife, sometimes more than we can handle," replied Bob, his exasperation apparent. "I've down-played this situation with command at the request of the mayor because we're all hoping it will settle down on its own."

Luke raised his eyebrows at that but Hammond appeared not to notice and carried on.

"Of course, Mayor Mutts can call in provincial conservation personnel from Port Alberni for a crisis situation, but there's no one who actually lives here in town except the wildlife conflict specialist for Parks Canada. That's Chelsea Kettle, she's alright. And while she's a federal employee like us, she's got her hands full most of the time with Park issues, which sometimes come with a strong dose of politics. Still, I've usually been able to get help from her when I've needed it in a real emergency."

Before Luke could ask what kind of "real emergency" pertaining to wildlife they had experienced, their conversation was cut short by a call about a brawl at one of the bars in town, all hands-on-deck.

However, he didn't let the exchange with the Sergeant weigh on his mind.

As he drove back to his motel, he realized he felt quite comfortable with his decision to make this place his home. Northern Newfoundland, with its winter-through-spring Arctic climate and polar bear issues, was a world apart from this rainforest terrain and seemed to be just what he needed to fix whatever it was that ailed him.

***

Over the next few weeks, however, Luke realized he'd under-estimated the landscape.

Not only did this little forest town have quite a few troublesome black bears, there were sly but lethal mountain lions, which the locals called cougars, and small packs of wolves—a real Trifecta of large predators.

But at least there weren't grizzlies, he thought to himself. He could do without those ancestors of polar bears, famous for their propensity for ferocious attack when their space was invaded, like the one that had taken Kate's husband.

Unfortunately, this sentimental notion that grizzlies would be the worst problem he'd ever have to face as a wildlife safety specialist would come back to haunt him later.

Chapter 5

Monday 18 December 4:00 pm

Luke's mind wandered erratically as he drove the twisting highway west towards the ocean. He was returning to Tofino after making a special shopping trip to Nanaimo, a small city on the east coast of the island he'd passed without notice when he'd first come to the Island.

He glanced in the rear-view mirror at the most impulsive large purchase he'd ever made. The 33-foot 5th wheel trailer was a different brand than Blake's but was otherwise quite similar. He'd picked one that was slightly lighter in weight and newer than hers but well below the maximum pulling capacity of his 10-year-old Chevy.

With all the bells and whistles, including a king-sized bed to accommodate his height, it was the most money he'd ever spent on a single purchase in his life. But it gave him a home he could take with him if he ever decided to leave, as Blake had pointed out when she'd talked him into buying it.

When Blake discovered her landlord had no rental properties that were available immediately, she'd brazenly asked if he'd mind if a friend shared the plot of land she was renting.

"I pointed out that the one-acre plot was plenty big enough for two trailers and said you'd pay to have a concrete pad installed and pay the same rent as I do, which would cover the extra service needed on the septic tank and garbage pickup. And he agreed that would work, especially since you're still technically on the job," Blake told him over the phone, slightly breathless with excitement.

"Without asking me if I even wanted to live in a trailer?" responded Luke, with barely concealed annoyance.

"Come on, Luke. You've lived in smaller cabins, you said so yourself. And we wouldn't be living together. We'd each have our own place. We'd just be neighbours."

"But Blake, those things are horrifically expensive!"

"On the face of it, yes. But you also said you'd be willing to buy a small house if you could find one, and a trailer would be way less expensive. It would eat into your savings, sure, but you wouldn't need a mortgage.

"Just look up the local dealers online," she continued. "There are lots of them on the island. Call around and see what kind of deal you can get if you pay cash. It might be the most realistic option for you right now. And I think I'd rather like having you as a neighbour after being out here on my own for so long with only Cooper for company."

So, he'd done as she suggested and found a good deal in Nanaimo. The whole idea had quickly grown on him the more he looked into it. And on the way into Nanaimo to pick up the trailer this morning, he'd realized he was feeling excited about the future for the first time in a very long while.

He'd had to spend several hours waiting for a trailer hitch to be installed on the truck, so he'd passed the time buying bedding and groceries in bulk to pick up on his way out of town.

Now, it was getting late in the day and he was trying to get through the worst of his journey back to Tofino before it got dark. The first part was what the locals called The Hump—the section of highway that went up and over the mountain range that ran down the centre of the island. One of the guys at the full-service gas bar Luke had pulled into on his way out of Nanaimo had given him a stern warning when he heard Luke was headed west.

"Nasty as hell after sunset with that snow on the road. You watch yourself pulling this new rig around those tight curves," he chided, as if Luke were an inexperienced tourist.

However, just like all the other Tofino residents, now he would have to traverse that road in all seasons for the myriad items local stores didn't keep in stock.

It had been a bad year for snow so far. Although he was used to snowy winters, there had apparently been much more snow than usual on the coast the month before he'd arrived and it hadn't really let up since then. On two occasions, accidents on The Hump and in the twisting and turning section that ran through Sutton Pass a bit further west, had briefly cut off this critical link connecting the west coast to the outside world. There was no other way in or out for Tofino inhabitants, except by boat or air.

Today, the high winds and blinding rain that had beset the coast a few days ago had morphed into a series of brief snow squalls up in the mountains. He'd had to again traverse the tight curves and steep slopes of The Hump between high berms of plowed snow but the road surface had recently been cleared and he soon put the hazard behind him. His truck was handling the added weight behind it with remarkable grace.

As he headed west towards the coast, he realized he hadn't thought about the consequences of making the long trip in one day. The twists and turns of the two-lane highway got more pronounced as it wound its way through the mountainous terrain. The swaying of the truck was oddly mesmerizing and he started to feel sleepy.

Shaking his head to wake himself up, he cracked his window open and played with the radio to find something to focus his mind.

Perhaps he should have stopped and bought a cup of coffee in Port Alberni, the sprawling mill town at the western end of The Hump. Its port designation came from its surprising location at the head of the Alberni Inlet, a long narrow fjord intruding 25 miles inland from the Pacific. But he'd been so eager to get back to Tofino, he'd pushed on through.

He was soon driving along the southern shore of Kennedy Lake, which had probably also been an ocean fjord at some time in its geological past. Approaching it from this direction, he remembered what Blake had told him about the section of highway up ahead.

"There was a bit that snaked really tightly through rock cliffs that went straight up the mountain on one side and way down to the lake on the other," she told him one night.

"After years of accidents and near-misses, a horrific crash finally got government officials off their asses about widening and straightening that stretch,"

"Do I really want to know?" he asked.

"An ambulance crew had been returning empty to Tofino in the middle of the night and the driver apparently fell asleep at the wheel. She missed one of the tight curves and drove right off a 100-foot cliff into the lake.

"No one was there to see her go over and the submerged rig wasn't spotted until hours later. By then, she and her male colleague had drowned—couldn't get out. He was asleep in the back, probably never realized what happened until it was too late. They still talk about it here—all the residents knew them. It just gutted the community.

"What came out during the inquest finally got the government to do something about the road. But it took years for them to get started, years longer than expected to finish, and the whole thing went way, way over budget. They did a ton of rock blasting, you'll notice if you look closely. It still looks like a raw wound on the mountain. And I'm not the only one who wonders if what's left is as stable as they claim—if maybe the engineers got a little carried away with the blasting."

Thinking back on that conversation, Luke sat up a bit straighter and paid closer attention than he had done going the opposite direction earlier in the day. Glancing up to his left, an enormously high cliff hinted at how much rock had had to be blasted away during the reconstruction.

Rounding one particular corner, protected now by a high concrete barrier piled high with snow, he glimpsed the lake briefly off to his right and far below. He wondered if this place had been where the ambulance had gone over. He'd noticed the spot the first time he'd driven the road to Tofino—in full daylight on a sunny day, it had been a spectacularly beautiful glimpse of scenery, but he hadn't known its history then.

Coming out of the new construction section meant he was getting close to the junction of this westbound highway and the north-south road that separated two disparate west coast communities. To the left and due south lay Ucluelet, a workers' town of loggers and commercial fishermen. To the right, at the far north end, lay Tofino—a tourist town of artisans and surfers that boasted a stunning variety of luxury resorts mixed with less sumptuous accommodation. The few commercial fishing boats still in residence were now overshadowed at the Tofino dock by visiting yachts and tour boats.

He turned north at the Visitor's Centre that marked the junction and headed through the dark, thick forests of Pacific Rim National Park, which lay prominently between the two towns. There had been no logging here for well over a century and much of it was as it had been hundreds of years before. The two longest beaches along that stretch of coast were protected within the Park boundaries and invisible from the highway, including most of the impressive 15-mile expanse of sand that made up Long Beach.

As a result, it wasn't until he'd passed the turnoff to the local airport on his right that he caught glimpses of the Pacific on his left. At the northern end of Long Beach, where the highway met the shore at Incinerator Rock, massive waves were crashing against the beach. However, all he saw in the low light was the white spray and foam the waves were generating on the shore. Being the only place to access the beach directly off the highway, there was a substantial parking lot, picnic area, and toilets used primarily by tourists. Even in this weather, at this time of day, he saw two vehicles pulled in.

But he didn't stop.

Somewhere out of sight on his right he knew lay the rabbit-warren of islands, protected inlets and quiet bays that separated the Esowista Peninsula from the main body of Vancouver Island—on his left, the Pacific roared ashore from Japan.

A few miles up the road, the heavy forest suddenly thinned and the elevation dropped, signalling he was out of the Park and into the Tofino Lowlands. This was the point where he'd almost turned back on his first trip in, after he'd spotted the 'tsunami zone' warning signs. He'd fought back his dread and reminded himself that while the west coast was at relatively high risk for tsunamis, it also had an excellent early warning system in place— something the east coast did not have, even after their recent disaster. Weeks later, he still had to remind himself to take a deep breath whenever he saw the sign.

Yet he knew it wouldn't be prudent to forget he'd now made his home along the Pacific 'Ring of Fire' where volcanic eruptions, earthquakes, and tsunamis had the last word.

The peninsula also visibly narrowed at this point and private land ownership became obvious as driveways intersected the highway. The biking path that connected Ucluelet with Tofino crossed the highway here and ran close to the road on the right instead of straight through the forest as it did inside the Park boundaries.

After driving past the now-familiar mix of tourist accommodation, gas stations, restaurants, and surf gear rental shops that intermittently disrupted the expanse of trees along both sides of the highway, he turned left at the road to Mackenzie Beach. The plot of land he would now share with Blake was at the far end of a gravel track that ran north off the beach access road, less than a mile from the highway but more or less parallel to it.

As he pulled into the short driveway, Luke breathed a quiet sigh of relief mixed with satisfaction. It had been a long time since he'd felt at home.

Earlier that week, he'd arranged to have someone pour a new concrete pad and pillar for his trailer. Blake had promised to help him tomorrow to get the rig set onto the pad and hooked up to septic, water, and power. But for tonight, he parked the ungainly unit on the most level spot he could maneuver into, deployed the slide-outs as he'd been shown, and prepared to spend his first night in his new home without detaching it from the truck.

Blake was still at work but had left on her outside lights. However, it was still dark and gloomy over on his side of the property. Inside, the trailer was a cozy refuge from the dark and wind, even if the only light came from a few candles and a battery-powered lantern.

Luke ate an unexciting supper of cold pizza and warm beer, made up the big bed with the new sheets, and fell into a deep slumber.

He didn't even hear Blake's truck roar up the driveway an hour later.

Chapter 6

Tuesday 19 December 4:00 pm

Blake and Luke sat with beers on her deck, surveying their handiwork in the fading light. After a full afternoon of effort, his trailer was now solidly installed and ready for permanent habitation.

"What are you doing for Christmas?" asked Blake as she got up to turn on her outside lights.

"I hadn't thought much about it," Luke replied, hoping she wouldn't catch the obvious lie. In fact, he'd been dreading the holiday season, knowing it would stir up memories of Kate and the first Christmas together that had unexpectedly been their last.

"Why don't we learn how to surf?" suggested Blake. "I haven't had the time or inclination since I got here but it might be fun to do it together. It'll be good for you, take your mind off things. I finish my last night shift that week, so after a morning sleep I'll be available the afternoon of Christmas Eve, Christmas Day, and Boxing Day. I went to see my family last summer during my holidays, so they won't be expecting me to come home.

"I'm sure I can find someone willing to give us a few lessons and we can rent the gear easily enough," she added. "It seems to be a popular time to be out on the waves so it will be a little crowded at the beach. But that probably means lots of novices around, so our ineptitude won't stand out."

Luke's benign expression as he listened to Blake's proposal turned into a scowl as she finished.

"You're assuming I'll be inept?" he asked, a hint of mock offense in his voice.

"I'm saying that surfing demands a certain skill set that I'm assuming you haven't mastered while living in the Arctic," she countered.

"Fair enough," he replied good-naturedly. "Definitely no opportunities for surfing in Resolute and if there was any surfing being done in Newfoundland, I never heard about it."

"So? What do you think?" Blake pressed.

"As long as we can have a big fire here afterwards. And no eggnog or turkey-and-mashed-potatoes nonsense. And no gifts."

"Done," agreed Blake. "But I draw the line at lights and tinsel. There needs to be a little brightness added, if nothing else. It's too dark otherwise. Not good for the soul."

After a moment's reflection, he nodded in agreement. They spent the rest of the evening discussing which of the half dozen or so local beaches to surf, deciding to wait and see what the waves and crowds were like when the time came.

***

Over the next two days, Blake spent the few hours of free time available festooning her outside deck with big silver snowflakes and bright red baubles, and replaced the strings of white lights with multi-coloured bulbs. Inside, she scattered a myriad of red and green candles of various sizes and shapes, and artfully arranged two strings of lights either side of the wood-burning stove. Given Luke's mood, she resisted adding more.

Luke spent a couple satisfying afternoons chopping some of Blake's ample firewood supply into manageable pieces for use in the outdoor firepit. Blake had an enormous domed screen for the firepit, custom built to avoid the risk of sparks setting off a wildfire but it certainly wasn't needed this time of year.

Luke lucked onto two photo shoots that week: a pre-Christmas wedding and a family reunion. There was only one more request for work over the holiday season, a wedding the day before Christmas. An incoming storm dictated they do the shoot before noon, which also meant it wouldn't interfere with their scheduled surfing lessons. Blake would be sleeping most of the morning anyway.

He was a bit disappointed at the paucity of jobs he had lined up, which probably meant he'd have to start promoting more aggressively. Lack of business meant he had more time on his hands than he'd expected before Christmas and he realized he missed the distraction Blake got from her job, a focus he'd had most of his adult life. For the first time, he wondered if this photography idea was going to work but tossed off the notion when he thought about the physical challenge Blake had set in place for the weekend and worried instead whether he was fit enough for surfing.

The first day on the water proved his point. Their teacher had them start their lessons at Long Beach, where the best waves were usually found. Both of them executed many inelegant falls during the first two hours, followed by spitting sea water and occasional cursing.

However, eventually Luke managed to get to his feet on the board and stay up for a few seconds before hurtling head-first into the surf. Spurred on by his success, Blake got the hang of the game after a few more tries, although just as briefly and with the same ultimate result.

Long before dark, they were both exhausted. Because they were relatively close to home, they opted to keep their wetsuits on and drove back to their trailer hide-away in Luke's truck before stripping down.

"I can see why an outside shower would be useful if you surfed every day," shouted Blake, shivering as she rinsed the sand off her wetsuit with a garden hose and then turned the hose on herself. "There's bloody sand in every crevice!"

"Surfing was your bright idea!" shouted Luke in reply. "Quit your complaining and get dressed so we can get the fire started and have a drink. And I think we've both earned a big steak."

***

"I'd call that successful Christmas avoidance, wouldn't you?" asked Blake the next afternoon, as she sat with Luke at the kitchen table, waiting for the chicken soup she'd made earlier to warm up on the stove.

"I do. And fun. It was incredibly cool to ride those waves, even if they were relatively small. It felt like a real accomplishment."

"I feel almost foolish for having waited so long to even try it," admitted Blake. "It seemed like a cliché but I've changed my mind. I believe I might enjoy being a local who surfs."

Luke got up to grab another beer out of the fridge and when he turned around, Blake was standing right in front of him. He met her gaze as she looked into his eyes and moved even closer.

Luke reached out to cup her jaw in his left hand and then leaned in to kiss her. Her lips responded greedily and then she threw her arms around his neck to pull her body into intimate contact with his.

He groaned with passion as he kissed her deeply and ran his hands through her hair and then down her back. Her heavy breathing spurred him on until his arms fell and he abruptly pulled away.

"I don't know whether this is such a good idea," he whispered breathlessly, still looking into her grey eyes with longing.

"You're over-thinking. It's an activity. Sort of a mutual prize for achieving a goal. A gold cup to each of us for gaining a little supremacy over nature," she whispered back while running her hand down his chest.

"Like celebrating a new skill by practicing one we've already mastered?" he responding, tilting his head and gifting her the cocky grin she knew so well.

"Yeah, like that," she whispered, entirely serious. "Just like that."

"Turn the soup off," he said decisively, taking her hand and turning towards the bedroom.

***

The meal did get eaten but not until several hours later.

Then they went back to bed. One thing led to another until they again lay entwined and exhausted.

"Feeling better?" asked Blake from the darkness beside him.

"I do, actually. Wait, was that pity sex?"

"No, not at all. More a self-serving treat with a touch of compassion, if you insist on a label. Kind of an engine jump-start. Don't try and pretend you didn't need it."

Luke's response was part grunt, part exasperated huff.

"You've been grieving long enough, Luke," Blake whispered. "It's time to let yourself move on. She'd understand."

"Yeah, you may be right," he finally replied.

Leaning over to kiss her on the cheek, he whispered, "thank you," in her ear.

Then he rolled over and muttered gruffly, "Now go to sleep."

Chapter 7

Sunday 24 December 4:10 pm

Calgary resident Gloria Perrez, whose family had come to celebrate Christmas in Tofino, drove up the steep hill and parked her car at the community centre where it intersected the Tonquin Trail. She got out and opened the back door to set her beloved Great Dane free.

It would be dark soon but the enormous dog needed a hard run before all the indoor festivities coming up or he'd drive them all crazy. Gloria had been warned by her father not to let the dog off his leash on the beaches. So, she'd opted for this remote forest trail above town that she'd read about in one of the tourist brochures, so she could let Zeus run free without anyone nagging her.

Setting off down the trail, in a hurry and distracted by the dog, she ignored the board full of maps and notices. As a result, she didn't see the one warning about the potential for encountering bears and wolves. Zeus raced off ahead of her and Gloria breathed a sigh of relief. She knew the trail was a relatively long hike downhill to a small beach but she didn't intend to go that far. Ten minutes in, ten minutes back would do the job if Zeus ran hard enough.

But it was darker and quieter than she expected as she got farther down the trail. As she walked, her sense of unease was replaced by what was surely a baseless fear. She tried to shake it off but couldn't help checking all around her every few seconds.

Far short of what she'd judged to be time to call Zeus back, the big dog came galloping up the hill towards her at full speed. Instead of circling around her as he usually did for a quick pat on the head, he continued on towards the parking lot as if his life depended on it.

Alarmed at what might have frightened him so much, Gloria stared into the darkness ahead of her, into a part of the path that was especially thick with trees. She didn't hear anything but vaguely made out a few dark shapes. However, she couldn't tell if there was something—or somebody—on the trail, or just overgrown bushes.

Then a slight movement gave her a glimpse of a dark animal with bright amber eyes.

Gloria froze. There was no sound and no further movement. Spooked, she slowly backed up the trail until it bent around a large tree and she could no longer see the path that led down to the beach. Then she turned and ran up the hill, checking behind her every few seconds, fully expecting to see the ghostly apparition following her. But there was nothing, and she soon slowed to a walk, too out of breath to go any faster.

Heart pounding and panting with exertion, she made it to her car to find Zeus sitting expectantly beside it. He jumped to his feet when he saw her and hopped right in when Gloria opened the back door. Quickly getting behind the wheel and starting the car, she breathed a sigh of relief when the automatic door locks clicked into place.

"What the hell? What on earth was *that*?" she asked the big dog, glancing at him as she backed out of the parking space. "Let's not stick around and find out, eh boy?"

She decided not to mention the encounter when she got back to the beach-front rental, knowing her father would condemn her choice of an off-leash walk in the woods. And that would upset her mother, who was already disappointed that there would again be no sunset for all of them to watch together.

For her mother's sake, she tried her best to be merry and bright throughout the long evening.

However, she woke with a start half-way through the night after a disturbing dream filled with shifting shapes and bright amber eyes. She wasn't sure if she'd screamed out loud or not, but no one came running so she figured probably not. It took her forever to get back to sleep because she couldn't get those eyes out of her mind.

In the morning, she was never so grateful to have the excuse of it being a holiday to tip a good measure of brandy into her coffee. After a second cup, the encounter in the woods finally started to retreat from her memory. She slept well the next night and then it was time to pack up and head home.

Oddly, Zeus hadn't seemed to mind being taken out only for short leash-walks over those two days—as if a walk around the block was all he'd ever required.

Chapter 8

The Christmas glow Luke had enjoyed after the time spent with Blake had lifted his spirits, which made him realize he was feeling antsy from lack of work. In the last two days, he'd done only two photo shoots, both of them so small they'd barely covered the cost of his Christmas surf gear rental.

This morning, he was headed for Wickaninnish Beach in the Park. Before Christmas, he'd left his business cards at a number of high-end tourist places, and last night he'd booked a major last-minute session with a wedding party who'd lost their photographer to a sudden attack of gallstones.

Luke spotted his party immediately as he turned into the parking lot. About twenty people milled around a beautiful blonde bride in a long, very tight-fitting white gown. The dress sported a princess-length train held aloft the asphalt by four overly-animated bridesmaids in matching orange gowns. Several young men in tuxedos mingled to one side, one of whom was probably the groom.

The group took up the space laid out for at least 30 cars and their loud exuberance made them impossible to miss.

The intentionality of the spectacle was evidenced by someone with a phone standing to one side, filming the choreographed disorder.

Luke approached the bride and introduced himself. After insisting last night on a fat, in-advance fee, he was prepared to be patient, gracious, and helpful to a fault.

"Oh my God, we're so grateful you were able to step in," cried the bride, hands to her head for added drama. "I don't know what we would have done without you."

"My pleasure," replied Luke calmly. "Let's head down to the beach and get set up."

Luke made sure that someone was responsible to carry out the inevitable make-up and hair touch-ups. He'd already learned the extent of havoc the wind played with carefully turned-out brides and their attendants, which they never seemed to anticipate. The more relaxed brides—those who'd sensibly planned a more rustic theme—took getting their hair messed up in stride. However, Luke sensed this one was not of that variety.

He sent the party down to the shoreline, which wasn't far away at this time of day. The groans of disappointment told him they hadn't bothered to check the tides when they'd planned the photos for early in the day, rather than later. However, given the forecast for afternoon showers, they might ultimately be happier with golden sand and deep blue sky in their memorable photographs than if they'd insisted on tidal expanses, which would inevitably have come with gun-metal grey surroundings and wet hair.

Luke wanted to get some wide-angle group shots, so he sent them further along the beach where he could get up onto the dunes that rose above the shore. This activity also helped loosen up their mood, as the assignment had the entire wedding party kicking along in the wave wash in bare feet and whooping like small children.

While they played, Luke struggled through the loose sand of the dunes to reach a favourable location. It had rained lightly overnight, so there was still a skin of dark wet sand in places the sun hadn't touched. Constantly checking back on the group to find the optimal spot for the shots he wanted, he stumbled over a log and almost fell.

Reminding himself to watch his footing more carefully, he noticed some animal tracks in the sand. These were much larger than the dog prints he was used to seeing and he stopped to look at them more closely.

Using his lens cap as a scale, he quickly took several photos of the prints before he realized the tracks led back into the scrubby bush that lay beyond—and that there were many more of them all around him.

"Surely wolf packs here aren't this big?" he muttered under his breath.

But before he could do any more wondering or recording, he heard a shout from the beach.

"Is this good?" yelled the groom. "My mum will be furious if we're late for lunch."

"Perfect!" replied Luke into the wind, holding both hands with thumbs-up.

He swivelled his focus back to the job at hand. He got the long shots he needed from his lofty perch before scrambling down for the close-ups on the beach itself, which took longer than he'd anticipated.

In the end, the party had had to make hasty apologetic phone calls on the way back to their cars to appease cranky relatives, and Luke had zero time for reflection on what he'd spotted on the dunes.

It wasn't until that night, as he sat preparing the photos to upload for his clients, that he remembered what he'd documented up on the dunes, including the last shot which showed the entire area covered in wolf tracks.

Chapter 9

Monday 1 January 12:35 am

A big New Years Eve bash was in progress on the edge of Chesterman Beach, organized by the new owners of the old Trudeau waterfront estate. It was a posh affair attended by elite sports stars and their followers, most of whom had arrived by plane earlier that day.

Just after midnight, property manager Ray Gibbs had retired to his cottage for a short break from the madness of the revelry going on around him.

"Rich folks and their parties!" he muttered to himself as he made a sandwich.

The dancing and drinking were still going strong up at the main house, which the catering and security staff had well in hand. His ongoing concern was a dozen or so youngsters who he suspected were slipping out of the guest house to smoke pot.

Half way through eating his snack, he heard a scream from the direction of the beach.

Shaking his head in resignation, he put down his sandwich and went out to see what was going on.

He hardly needed his extra-bright torch, since the light of the full moon revealed the suspected pot smokers making their way up from the beach.

Two scantily-clad girls half staggered, half ran past him on his left, falling over several times until one off them vomited into a patch of brush.

Gibbs grabbed a hulking young man, big enough to be a football linebacker, who'd almost run over him in panic.

"What the hell's going on!" the manager demanded, giving the wide-eyed boy a shake. "Slow down and tell me what happened. Is someone hurt?"

"Someone decided to go for a swim," the huge kid explained as he struggled to control his breathing. "Most of us thought it was too cold so we just hung out and watched. Shay went down the beach a bit and sat near the edge of the water, even though she kept having to move up as the tide came in.

"A wolf just walked up to her and stood there, looking at her. She starting talking to it for the longest time, gibberish, you know, like she was trying to make friends. It kept coming a little bit closer, like it was starting to trust her.

"For some reason, she stood up then and the wolf bolted in and grabbed the bottom of her pants, tugging at it. I guess Shay thought it wanted to play, so she bent over and put her hands out—like she was going to pet it, you know?—and it grabbed the sleeve of her jacket.

"That's when Kelsey yelled that there were more of them further down the beach. Wolves, I mean. At first, they were all just standing there but then they started to walk slowly towards Shay and the wolf tugging at her sleeve. Shay was sort of laughing and crying at the same time, so it was hard to tell if she was scared or not. Then she screamed. I went with Kelsey and Xander—they're both even bigger than me—to see if she was OK, and the wolf let go of her jacket.

"I realized then that there were wolves near me as well because they started snarling. Jesus, that really freaked me out! I yelled at everyone to run. But no one moved. Kelsey and Xander picked up some big sticks—small logs almost—off the beach and started swinging them around at the wolves until they backed off."

"How the hell much dope did you guys smoke?" Gibbs said with a smirk, shaking his head. "What's your name, anyway?"

"My name's Brad and yeah, those guys have been smoking some but Kelsey and I don't do drugs. I don't think Xander had any either. There really *were* wolves," the kid insisted. "You can go and see for yourself, there'll be wolf tracks all over."

"Brad, you just get your friends and go back to the guest house," Gibbs demanded loudly. "And stay there. No more swimming or late-night walks on the beach. None of you are in any shape to be outside after all the drinking and smoking you've been doing. And don't be scaring the rest of the guests with your ridiculous stories about making friends with wolves!"

He then watched until the entire group had made their way off the beach, some grumbling, some crying. He shook his head in disgust as he watched their backs move towards the main part of the estate.

"Idiot stoners!" he exclaimed, looking out over the water.

Out of curiosity, he took a stroll down to the water's edge but didn't see a single wolf track. He admitted to himself that even if there had been paw prints in the sand, the tide was coming in so fast they would be underwater by now, but the kid's story was nevertheless too outlandish to be believed.

He headed up to the main house to let the boss know the stoner kids had concocted some nonsense story about seeing wolves on the beach to scare everyone. That would put an end to it.

Chapter 10

Tuesday 2 January 7:20 a.m.

Cox Bay resident Tyrone Stark walked right past the sign in the parking lot warning people not to walk dogs off-leash without even looking at it. He'd long ago dismissed such warnings as propaganda. He'd never believed the stories in the local newspaper about wolves attacking dogs on other beaches.

Tyrone had convinced himself Parks Canada officials made up these stories. He'd never known any local who'd experienced such an attack but then, he seldom talked to his neighbours and never went to town meetings. Having lived on the edge of the Park his whole life, he was sure officials really wanted to ban dogs from the Park entirely but knew the public would never accept it. So, they'd resorted to scare tactics to stop people from letting their dogs run on the beach.

This morning, it was barely light but brightening every minute as he walked south along the edge of the wave-wash in the fog. No one else in sight at this end of the beach. His three young, mixed-breed dogs preferred running along the hard-packed wet sand left by the receding tide, which today gave them a huge expanse of beach to traverse. He knew the dark forest was out there somewhere on his left but couldn't see it.

He ambled along without purpose then suddenly raised his head. Up ahead, one of the dogs had yelped in alarm and all three of them were now running frantically towards him. That's when he noticed a huge pack of wolves swarming out of the woods.

The wolves quickly overtook the dogs and surrounded them. Every time one of the dogs tried to bolt free, without a sound the pack cut it off and then tightened its noose.

At first, Tyrone was speechless and paralyzed with fear. When he finally gathered his resolve and took a few steps forward to intervene, the two wolves nearest him advanced, snarling, until he backed away.

Soon, all the dogs could do was fight for their lives.

You could hardly call it a battle. It was over so quickly the weak cries of the dogs were swallowed by the fog. The wolves silently dragged the bodies into the forest and disappeared.

Tyrone stood there for the longest time, struggling to understand what he'd just seen. Shaking his head, he stared off into the fog, calling the dog's names frantically even as he knew it was pointless.

Finally, he walked dejectedly back along the beach toward the parking lot where he'd left his jeep, looking back over his shoulder every so often. He told himself he couldn't really have seen what he thought he'd seen. The dogs must have simply run off—caught the scent of a deer or something, and got lost.

No one would have noticed him return home pet-less.

But he missed them. And he missed his walks on the beach, which he'd stopped doing now they were gone.

So, at the end of the week, he drove east to Nanaimo and bought a pair of tough-looking pit bulls from someone anxious to get rid of them. They seemed nice enough dogs.

He barely noticed that he never again chose to walk with them in the fog or the darkness of very early morning.

Chapter 11

Thursday 4 January 10:10 am

On his way to the local bakery for a quick breakfast, Luke literally bumped into an old woman. She hurried out the door of a small neighbouring shop so fast she collided with his shoulder.

Dressed in clean clothes and with freshly-washed hair, he almost didn't recognize her. He knew he'd seen her several times before, slowly pedalling a red-and-rust fat-tired mountain bike with a big rear carrier along the road to Mackenzie Beach. She always had a big black dog patiently trotting behind her, and had guessed she was a local.

A scowl flashed across her face as she ducked out of his way. She disappeared quickly around the corner, as if not wanting to be seen. No dog though, which seemed odd. He'd never seen her without it.

Curious, he popped into the shop she'd just emerged from, which he hadn't yet explored. It was an art gallery of sorts that appeared to sell sculptures and paintings.

"Good morning," chirped the small, gray-haired woman behind the counter near the front door. "Have a look around and let me know if I can help explain any of the pieces. All of the art here is done by local artists and can't be found anywhere else in Canada."

"Thank you," replied Luke. "I'm actually not so much interested in the art as the woman who was just in here. My name's Luke Robinson, by the way, I'm new in town," he said warmly, offering his hand. "I've come from Newfoundland and I'm doing specialty event photography."

"I'm Betsy Bennett, the owner," she replied, sliding her small, warm hand into his much larger one. "Welcome! I've had this little shop for four decades, so I'm kind of an old-timer. I never really wanted to move here, you know, so I started it as a kind of side-venture to my husband's restaurant, just to have something for myself. I sold off his place after he died. I never did have much interest in feeding people. Working here keeps me as busy as I need to be and I like meeting people."

She plucked one of her business cards out of a holder on the counter and passed it over to Luke, who nodded in satisfaction. He offered her one of his own from his pocket before adding hers to his stash. Both were a similar, simple style on a white background, without the flash he had come to expect from younger entrepreneurs.

"I've seen that woman around, but never quite so spiffed up as she was today," commented Luke. "I don't mean to be rude or nosy but I think she must live near me and wondered if you could tell me a bit about her."

"Oh sure, that's Baylou. No last name, as far as I know, and to be honest, I doubt if that's even her real name.

She's one of my artists, actually one of my original artists, and probably the oldest. We made an agreement, eons ago, that she'd try to make herself a bit more presentable than usual when she comes to the gallery to drop off her pieces."

She gestured to a stunning clump of twisted driftwood about two feet tall beside her on the counter. It was polished smooth and intricately studded with bits of mother of pearl, animal teeth, and scraps of copper, some of which were hammered, others smooth and shiny. Two smaller pieces, each with uniquely inlaid patterns made from scrap metal and ceramic beads sat beside it.

"Baylou usually brings me a few pieces every month or so. I like to keep at least ten in the gallery at all times. They sell quite well, even in winter. This over-sized piece is about as large as she produces, and surprisingly those sell the best, even though they're of course the most expensive."

"Do you know where she lives? I'm staying in a place off Mackenzie Beach Road and I think she must live fairly near there."

"Yes, that's right. Baylou has an old cabin on the other side of the highway, just south of you. Big chunk of woods off Sharp Road. You must know it, it's the one that takes you down to the Mud Flats on the east side.

"There's no road to her place. She has to hike in and out. I believe she usually takes a trail to a spot on Hellesen Road where she stashes her bike. Then she either rides the bike path into town or crosses over the highway to get to the south end of Mackenzie Beach. Apparently, she sometimes rides into the Park along the bike path or so other people have said. I've never seen her there myself."

"I didn't see her dog with her outside. Does she usually leave him at home when she brings in her pieces?"

"No, that dog's always with her, I've never minded having him here, always well behaved. I noticed it too, that she didn't have him today. When I asked her about him, she was quite short with me. Rude, I thought."

"What did she say?"

"Just said, 'murdered'. Just like that, in a real low, flat voice. No explanation. And when I asked her what happened, she muttered something about howling wolves and then walked out without saying goodbye."

"That *is* a bit strange," offered Luke. "How long has she lived here?"

"Oh, it seems like forever, but longer than me. She's definitely older than me, she must be 80 or nearly so. Not many of those around anymore. She told me once she'd come to town as a teenager and never left. Took part in the old growth protests in '93, along with a number of other locals. My husband and I came soon after that to start a restaurant, so she'd been here for ages by that time. I told him no one wanted southern-style BBQ in a town with so many vegetarians but would he listen? Of course not!"

"Wow, I'm surprised she's managing so well at her age," Luke replied, ignoring the restaurant comment.

"How on earth was she able to buy property here? Even I couldn't find something affordable!"

"I think someone gave her that shack in the woods—a local hippie couple who'd come here soon after the highway was paved. I'm sure she wouldn't have had the money to buy it otherwise. There were all kinds of odd things going on during the protests, most of them kind of got swept under the rug and no one asked questions. You know how it is."

"I do indeed," admitted Luke.

"Baylou has always lived on the edge, from what I can tell. People tell me things, but she keeps to herself. In the early days she said she sometimes sold some wood carvings on commission at a shop in Ucluelet, way before my time. Her skill with the driftwood sculptures only really developed as the town became better known in the late 90s. Now she supports herself from her art alone, I think. She doesn't even get a government old age pension as far as I know. It's not a fancy life, for sure, but she seems content enough with it."

"So, when I've seen her riding along the beach road, she must be off collecting driftwood," Luke mused aloud.

"Not always. She's complained off and on that it's harder now to find good pieces, with so many people combing the beaches. But she's got a few favourite spots where wood tends to collect after a storm, so she's quite strategic in her searching. Most days, she's just off for a long ride along the beach with Junior. It's part of their routine. Most of the time, it's as close as she gets to people."

"I wonder what she'll do without him," pondered Luke, thinking of Kate and how attached she had been to her big dog. "The dog, I mean."

"I think she'll be fine," replied Betsy. "She never had a dog before Junior. Someone dumped him as a puppy near her place and she rescued him. I think she eventually came to like having him around, to be honest, but I don't think she was ever really a dog-lover, not like some people around here."

"Yeah, there do seem to be quite a few of those," said Luke. "Lots of dogs on the beaches, I've noticed."

"Dogs on the beaches have been an issue here for ages," Betsy said, shaking her head. "I'm not a real beach-goer, I got over that obsession years ago. But I do go to town meetings. Even when my husband and I first moved here, there was a huge divide between people who thought dogs on the beach should be leashed up—or even banned outright—and those who wanted to let their dogs run free. It used to be that tourists coming here were terrified to walk along the trails because they were terrified of cougars and bears, so they'd stick to the beaches. These days, even the beaches aren't safe—because of the wolves—and still we have folks that simply refuse to stop letting their dogs running lose."

"I'd heard black bears and cougars caused most of the problems around here," replied Luke.

"Oh, it certainly was true for most of the time I've lived here. We still have recurring bear trouble, alright. Late summer and fall, usually. Some years are worse than others depending on how the berries and salmon are doing, and how well folks take care of their garbage. Big cats, now—they have their own schedule of troublemaking, although now that I think of it, less so in recent years than when I first moved here."

"I'm impressed that you are so knowledgeable about problem wildlife," said Luke, with genuine awe.

"Well, you have to be, don't you—dealing with tourists all the time? I talk to all kinds of people, really, locals as well as tourists and repeat visitors. What I mean is that lots of folks come here to stay for weeks on end every year and bring their pets with them. Regular visitors, you know? Not typical tourists. But still no idea how dangerous wild animals can be.

"Cougars around here take house cats and small dogs, whatever they can get their teeth into. Cunning devils, they are. They'll stalk you through the woods. You never know they're there until they attack from behind. Kids are especially at risk. Locals know not to let little ones run too far ahead on the trails. We've had fatal attacks, though as I said, none recently."

"I've never lived in a place that had cougars," admitted Luke. "I've dealt with big bears but never big cats."

"Not really the time of year just now, we don't usually have cougar trouble during the winter. Summer's a different story."

"But what about the wolf issue?" Luke asked. "You said they're more of a problem now than they used to be. What exactly do you mean by that?"

"Well, as I said, people tell me things. I'm not a gossip, but people seem to see me as a neutral party. I don't really understand why but they say things here they wouldn't say anywhere else. Even locals."

"Like what, exactly?" asked Luke, pressing for more details.

"Well, a lot of it revolves around those pamphlets Parks Canada folks keep leaving with me," she said, turning to point to the counter which held a stack of the same brightly-coloured pamphlets Sergeant Hammond had shown him when he was at the detachment.

"Someone will pick one of those up, flip through it, and then tell me about a frightening encounter they've just had with wolves somewhere around town or in the Park. Usually, they'll admit they haven't told anyone else about it. Even if I encourage them to report it to Park officials or the RCMP, they say—and this is their words, every time—they don't want to get the wolves in trouble. One woman came in, years ago now, after two wolves ambushed her in a parking lot at dusk. She was able to take refuge in one of those change rooms—scared silly she was, waited hours in there to make sure they were gone—still wouldn't tell anyone. She's the one really got me thinking, kind of keeping track. I'd say it's been bad, off and on, for at least 10 years. But I've heard even more of these stories in the last few months than even last year at this time, for sure."

"So, you're suggesting more confrontations with wolves are going on right now than officials in town or the Park are even aware of?" Luke asked, genuinely surprised. "And you haven't said anything to any of them?"

"Not really my place, is it? And it's not just me keeping quiet. I'm almost positive Parks people know more than they're saying. I had someone in here last week saying a ranger came to their campsite during the day—just chatting, you know how they do—and offered them free bear spray. Because this person had said they were afraid to walk on the beach after hearing about someone else's wolf encounter. I know the Park's pamphlet says it's advisable to carry bear spray to protect against wolves but this business of rangers handing bear spray out for free has never happened before, or I'm sure I'd have heard about it."

"Wow," said Luke. "I agree, that sure sounds like the Park may have a bigger problem with wolves than they're letting on."

"Not just the Park," Betsy countered. "In town as well, all around really. If you think about it, if a wolf killed Baylou's dog, there's probably others no one is reporting as well. There's such a reverence for wolves in this town that most people are very reluctant to say anything."

"That's concerning, I agree. I'll keep that in mind," Luke replied, trying to remember why he'd come in to the gallery to being with. "And thanks for telling me about Baylou, Betsy. I hope I get a chance to talk to her sometime."

"Well, she's not usually much of a talker, but you never know. She's managed a conversation with me on occasion, when she's in the mood. Folks around here think she's gone a little crazy living alone for so long, or claim she's a drunk or senile. I don't know, she's always seemed perfectly sane to me, just private and shy. I know she drinks but she's never been drunk when she comes in here."

"Does she have any friends?"

"She's mentioned a kid named Willie from time to time in the last little while. His grandfather Tom Moses works at the Tin-Wis Resort over where the old residential school used to be on Mackenzie Beach—you must know the place. You can't miss it. Very successful First Nations tourist outfit, run mostly by local band members that live nearby."

"Yes, I've noticed the place, looks quite nice," said Luke.

"Baylou told me she'd known several people that worked there, from way back when it first opened. But there were a number of deaths among the band members that ran the resort, some natural, some tragic, over the last few years. Then, year-before-last, Willie's father took over the top management position. Willie is about 10 years old, I think, maybe a bit older. I believe his grandfather runs the interpretive program there. Willie spends a lot of time on the beach, she said. I think that's where she meets him."

"Ah, I'll have to watch for them. I haven't spent much time so far on my own beach, too busy exploring the others for my business. But thanks so much for all this information Betsy, it's been a pleasure meeting you. I hope we run into each other again soon."

"Likewise, Luke. If I hear of anyone looking for a photographer, I'll send them your way. Best of luck."

Lost Dog

In another place, at another time...

Julie's father slowed for the turn and pulled the car onto the gravel road leading to Englishman River Falls Provincial Park. Bill Tanner was irritated by his wife Brenda's insistence that they stop here to let the dog stretch its legs and pee but turned as she directed nevertheless.

Julie Tanner was 12 years old and her brother Ivan was 7, and it was the summer of 1993.

The children were already groggy after the short drive from the ferry that had taken them from Vancouver to Nanaimo, and Bill had hoped they would sleep through the long drive ahead to Tofino. They'd gotten worn out being on a ferry for the first time, racing up and down the decks in the fresh salt air.

He worried a stop now would simply wind them up again, but on second thought, realized it might just exhaust them further and make a long nap in the back seat afterwards a sure thing instead of a possibility.

Pepper, Julie's young German Shepherd, paced excitedly in the cargo area of the station wagon. She seemed to have sensed that the change of speed when the car turned might mean a full stop and almost certainly picked up the word 'walk' from the human conversation in the front of the car.

Julie did as well. As Pepper paced, Julie began to rouse from her torpor. Taking the dog for a walk in the park would be her job, something she took seriously.

Before getting the big black dog, Julie had been quite withdrawn and bookish. She had made no new friends after they had moved out of their old neighbourhood but raising Pepper from a puppy had brought her out of her shell. She actually did walk and feed it every day, trained it, brushed it and cleaned up the messes, as she'd promised she would.

Watching Julie bloom, Bill knew he'd been right to support her plea for the dog against his wife's objections but willingly admitted, at least to himself, that the resulting family friction was partly his fault.

Julie had done all of the reading about dog behaviour and training but often got vetoed on decisions by Brenda, who knew nothing about dogs. A power struggle of sorts had developed over Pepper. Brenda thought Julie was over-thinking things and demanding too much control, refusing to let the dog be a dog. Pepper was an exuberantly dominant female and Julie had her hands full.

Most of the time she made good progress but Brenda undermined her training regularly enough that the dog was less well behaved than she should have been, given that she was almost two years old. The bad behaviour infuriated Julie. The most irksome trait was that Pepper often didn't come when she was called. She preferred to goad Julie into a merry chase first, which the entire family knew well.

As a result, Julie was instantly enraged when she climbed out of the car to see her mother had beat her to the back of the car, whereby she had quickly lifted the rear cargo door and let Pepper leap out without putting a leash on her first. Of course, she bolted away to the edge of the parking lot to pee, raced around the ten cars that were there, and then ran down the path towards the waterfall.

"What did you do that for?" she shouted at her mother. "Why didn't you put her leash on?"

"Don't worry, Julie," said her father, trying to calm his daughter down before she got to the name-calling stage of outrage, but not before shooting his wife a withering look. "We'll get her back."

They locked up the car and headed down the path, all of them calling desperately for the dog. At one point, Julie thought she saw Pepper up ahead but she couldn't catch up with her no matter how fast she ran. She never did see her after that; none of them did.

Once they got near the place where the path intersected the river, the sound of the waterfall became deafening. It was late spring and the runoff from the snowpack in the mountains had swollen the river high up on its banks. The falls were spectacular, more impressive than Julie had expected. But more important, the violently rushing water made so much noise that she instantly realized Pepper would never hear them calling if she was anywhere nearby.

"She's gone!" she sobbed as she fell into her father's arms. "She can't hear us!

She turned on her mother and shouted, "It's your fault and now I'll never get her back!"

Julie ran back to the car and the rest of the family followed more slowly behind, Brenda taking up the rear with a show of mild contrition.

When they got to the car, Bill told them to get in while he examined a notice board.

"There isn't any point in us staying here looking any longer," he said in the most soothing voice he could muster. "We have to leave now or we won't get to Tofino before dark. But we'll let the park ranger here know what happened and if anyone finds Pepper they'll know who to call. And we'll stop on our way back and look again."

They did stop on the way home but the result was the same: no Pepper. The ranger said no one had seen her. It was like she had disappeared into thin air. Julie was heartbroken and the rift between her and her mother widened noticeably.

Bill kept calling the park ranger all summer long and finally, in August, there was some news. Someone had seen a black female Shepherd just like Pepper, hanging out with a male wolf. The pair had been successfully hunting deer.

"She's gone wild," the ranger concluded. "But as long as the two of them don't get into the habit of killing livestock, your dog will likely survive. But there's really no chance of getting her back now.

"Tell your daughter I'm sorry it ended up this way. Dogs go missing more often than you'd think. However, most lost dogs starve to death or get killed by bears, or shot by farmers when they try to kill sheep or chickens. So really, this situation is the best outcome imaginable short of getting her back.

"Believe me, it doesn't happen very often. This is the first I've heard of a dog taking up with a wolf. Most dogs are too submissive to partner with a wolf and the wolf kills them. But at least she's alive out there and probably happy enough. Who knows, she may even have a litter or two of pups with that wolf."

Chapter 12

Friday 5 January 2:30 pm

Peggy Marcus sighed heavily as she finished feeding the remaining chickens, later again than she'd intended. She was tired all the time now because of her pregnancy but was increasingly terrified as well.

Ian had only been gone for a few days. She missed him terribly of course but they needed the money from this short-term job too desperately for him to pass it up.

He'd wanted to turn it down, of course. When the offer came in to do some architectural drawings for an old client of his—who always paid well, she reminded him— he had shrugged it off.

"I can't, Peg. You're already six months along. I can't leave you to take care of everything for three weeks. Never mind about the money, we'll get by somehow."

"Ian, I love that you want to stay and protect me but please don't. I know you're not thrilled about going back to drawing plans and hate the thought of being back in Vancouver. But the money you'll earn from just a few weeks away won't just get us through the winter, it will really set us up for success this summer."

Taking his hands in hers, she pleaded with him.

"Please go, love. I can hold things together while you're gone. I promise I won't do too much. I have Pete to call on if I need help, and I'll ask Jenny to stay up at the house with me while you're gone."

That had sealed the deal but now she shook her head at her persuasiveness. Maybe she shouldn't have worked so hard at convincing him to go.

Jenny had arrived at the back door of the house just after the Remembrance Day weekend in November. They'd reopened only on weekends after the October blizzard on a trial basis but without their usual staff it had been more taxing than they'd expected. She and Ian had been arguing about whether to continue opening weekends until the staff returned in March or just keep the doors closed.

"Are you Peggy? Betsy at the gallery said you might have work and a place to stay. My name's Jenny Harris. I can cook, clean, whatever you need."

Peggy looked intently at the tall, dark-haired young woman. She looked strong enough.

"How are you with livestock? Horses, goats, and pigs, I mean, not cattle."

"Well, I took riding lessons for two summers years ago, so I know the basics of looking after horses. I expect I can learn about the others. I like all animals, generally speaking, although I'm not crazy about chickens. There's just something about birds that freak me out."

"You likely won't like the emus then either. But that's OK, they don't take much looking after, I can deal with them and the chickens myself. How about chopping wood?"

"I love chopping wood," Jenny replied with a warm smile.

Peg held out her hand.

"I'm Peg. Come on in."

Jenny followed Peg into a homey-looking kitchen, which was warm and smelled strongly of yeast. She glanced around but didn't see any bowls filled with rising dough or loaves of freshly-baked bread. She settled into a worn wooden chair at the big central table and watched Peg as she made tea.

A big, battered kettle sat at the ready on the back of a massive wood stove and Peg deftly shifted it to a hot spot at the front. The water quickly came to a boil and Peg poured the steaming liquid into a teapot decorated with big pink roses and covered the pot with a quilted cozy.

She sat the hot tea on the table beside a jug of milk and sugar bowl that matched the teapot. She reached behind her to lift two clean mugs off hooks mounted in an open cupboard and fished two teaspoons out of a drawer. She handed a cup and spoon to Jenny and set the other in front of herself.

"Maybe I should go first," said Peg, a little breathlessly. "Then you'll know if you're interested in staying any longer than it will take to drink your tea."

"Betsy only said you'd let your staff go for the winter but might need some extra help on weekends now because of your pregnancy," Jenny interjected. "I saw some goats on the roof of a shed as I came in and noticed a menu offering hot soup, fresh bread, and muffins. How much more is there?"

"Well, let's see. We have pony rides in good weather, so there are half a dozen Shetlands for that. The two miniature horses are all for show, they're too delicate to ride. In the summer, we sell ice cream but soup moves better in the winter months. Tourists just love the goats on the ice cream shed! I know we kind of stole the idea from that place in Coombs but what can I say? It's a huge draw and you use what works. Right now, there are 18 goats, which is more than we really need, to be honest.

"We also sell small handicrafts made by local artists. Not gallery-quality stuff like Betsy carries, but ear-rings, necklaces, candles, fancy soap, that sort of thing.

"There's a petting zoo of sorts in the summer with baby goats, chicks, and the piglets that our two pot-bellied pigs produce every year. The two donkeys pull a cart around the property for kids too young or too scared to ride the ponies. When they aren't working, we keep the donkeys in with the horses for company and protection in the far paddock during the day.

"The emus and fancy chicken breeds are all for show. They really aren't much trouble and the emus are exotic enough that folks tend to stick around watching them. We figure the longer people stay on the property, the more they spend. Our aim is to have enough things to do to keep visitors busy for two or three hours in the summer, an hour or so in the winter.

"Oh, and there's Big Ben, our black Shire gelding. Original name, right? But it's one people remember and that's the important thing. Even when it's too cold and wet for riding, people love to take selfies with the miniature horses next to such a big draft horse. Folks are all about the photos, which is actually great because some of them post on social media and that's free advertising!

"If the weather isn't too bad, we hook Ben up to a narrow carriage Ian custom-built last winter that fits on some of the local trails and hire them out for special occasions.

"Some years have been better than others for the pony rides and ice cream versus the handicrafts and hot soup, but overall, we've been able to survive by diversifying. This year is our fifth winter.

"We were only able to buy the property because my mother died and left me enough to pay cash for it. No one would have been able to afford a mortgage for something like this. It was originally a botanical garden of some sort and then a First Nations conservation centre. But for some reason—they never did tell us why—the band decided to sell out and move their centre onto Meares Island.

"We were lucky. We just happened to show up at the right time with enough cash to buy the entire 12 acres, including the dock out into the Mud Flats, which you can't see from here. We had just enough left over to do all the renovations we needed and of course, to purchase all the animals. But we were sure we could make the business work. However, it's been more difficult than we anticipated.

"First of all, it turned out to be not the greatest time to start a new business, especially this one. Mind you, a lot of businesses in town have had a few rough years. The three guest houses that were our nearest neighbours all went under last fall after struggling for years. For some reason, this September was great but then the road closures because of the snow in October brought everything to a standstill.

"We had to lay off our regular staff much earlier than before, except for Pete, our farm manager. He and my husband Ian wanted to close up completely for November and December but decided we should try limited openings in hope that the trade over the Christmas and New Year's weekends especially will make it worthwhile. So, that's the plan: open weekends only as long as we can.

"We'll have all the staff back full time by early March and will open full time then, but right now we could really use an extra hand. Especially if you can bake muffins and bread on weekends as well as muck out a barn now and then during the week. As you might guess by my size, I'm expecting twins and simply don't have the energy I did even last month. There's a small commercial kitchen set up in the next room, where I've got some bread going."

"I thought I smelled bread!" said Jenny. "I have more than 10 years experience as a line cook in a busy hotel kitchen, so I'm sure I can manage a few days of making soup, muffins and bread. And I'd be more than happy to help out with the animals."

"Why are you here?" asked Peg, pouring herself more tea. "Middle of November is an odd time to come looking for work in Tofino."

"I came here for a long weekend holiday with my friend Julie Tanner, who's been coming to Tofino on vacation for decades. I'd never been before and I enjoyed it so much that a few days just didn't seem like enough time. Julie had to go back for her job in Nanaimo but I'm currently out of work. The hotel I've been cooking for over the last few years finally went under. I had enough savings to stay on for another few weeks but when Betsy said you might have a short-term job for a cook as well as a place to stay, I thought I might stay a while longer. If you'd have me, that is."

"For now, I can only pay you for two days a week with full room and board, just until my staff return in early March. And we absolutely need you to stay over the Christmas-New Years stretch, that's going to be critical."

"I think I can make that work. I'll have to sublet my apartment in Nanaimo while I'm here but I have a friend who would probably be interested."

Peg took Jenny for a tour around the property and introduced her to Ian and Peter. Big Ben took to her right away and Taffy, their most cantankerous Shetland, allowed her chin to be scratched without threatening to bite. That sealed the deal for Peg, and after a subtle nod from Ian, she showed Jenny to the bunkhouse.

It had been almost two months now since Jenny had arrived at the door and Peg knew they wouldn't have managed without her. Peg had become even more enormous shortly after Jenny joined them. The babies weren't due until the end of March if she managed to carry them to term, which she'd been warned might be wishful thinking.

Last week, Peg had admitted she was a little freaked out about the prospect of juggling two newborns with the spring business workload, even with full staffing in place. With some coaxing, Jenny had agreed to stay on as long as she was needed, even if that meant staying through the summer.

So, when Ian left for Vancouver to take up his drawing gig, Jenny had moved into the guest room up at the house. It was tiny but she insisted she didn't mind. She helped Peg get the nursery ready and the two women quickly fell into an easy camaraderie.

The issue of the disappearing livestock was something the two women never discussed when Ian was around but one evening over tea the day after he'd left, Jenny asked Peg what they were going to do about the wolves.

"What if they come back?" she asked in a quiet voice, knowing Peg would realize instantly what she was talking about.

"I really don't know, Jenny," she answered, shaking her head. "I hope like hell they don't, at least before Ian gets home."

Over the last few weeks, they had lost the two emus and half of the chickens to wolves. Ian and Pete said to keep quiet about it, which Jenny agreed to do after the situation had been explained. The business had lost three chickens the summer before to a cougar, Peg told her, which had freaked the staff out, but luckily for everyone, the big cat had been captured and relocated the following day. As business had been brisk at that time of year, the incident was soon forgotten.

However, at dusk on the evening before Ian left, they had lost one of the pigs and realized that the attacker wasn't one wolf but several. Jenny and Peg had exchanged nervous glances over the carnage within the hog fence but neither spoke up when Ian insisted they tell no one.

"I'll buy a gun on my way back from Vancouver," he conceded. "You know I hate to do that but we need some way to fight back. I won't have them coming after the horses."

After the attack on the pig, Jenny had asked Pete why Ian was so adamant that no one know about the wolves. Pete had been with the business since its start-up and Jenny had learned she could ask him things she dare not bring up with Peg.

"Because he doesn't want to lose the business. When they applied for a license, Ian and Peggy were warned by city council that so much livestock would attract predators. But because of the new approach to issuing permits, they were allowed to proceed as long as they had a viable plan in place to deal with potential predators. So, Ian had a sturdy barn built for the horses, and a separate building for the goats to stay in overnight.

"He also had to install electric fencing around the emus, chickens and pigs, which was a huge expense. But it turned out the system fails spontaneously for reasons we still haven't figured out, and of course it goes down whenever we lose power completely during a storm, which happens more often than you'd think. Even with generator back-up, it isn't fool-proof.

"Ian won't admit any of this to anyone. Partly it's pride, of course, the 'we told you so' factor. But there's also the very real possibility the business could be shut down if the town council finds out that wolves have been killing their animals. The council says they have to take a tough stance when protective measures fail because any predator that finds any easy food source will keep coming back. Predators near town puts the entire community at risk."

"Why would that be?" asked Jenny, truly puzzled.

"Because predators learn quickly. Once they've been successful killing livestock at one location in town, they'll keep trying out other places nearby to see what else they can get away with. The town has had problems with cougars and bears forever, of course, but the problem with wolves is more recent."

"I understand Ian's position," he continued. "But I still think he should have had a gun on site from the beginning. And he says folks in town and the tourists that support us are so enamoured of wolves that he would be crucified for killing one, even if it came after the livestock. He thinks we're in a no-win situation with the wolves and he may be right.

"But I wonder how long it will take before he changes his mind. He's really come to love these animals, especially the horses. It would really gut him if anything happened to one of them. I'm really afraid now that things will get worse before they get better."

Chapter 13

The incessant rain overnight had now stopped, probably briefly by the look of the clouds on the horizon. Baylou had been up early and spent the morning cleaning out the chicken coop. When she woke from an after-lunch nap, she headed to the beach. It had been almost a month since his death but it still felt strange not to have Junior trailing behind her like a shadow.

She rode slowly along the wet sand above the wash of the falling tide. As she passed the rows of Quonset-style cabins that dominated the beach-front landscape at the south end of the beach, she glanced ahead and noticed a lone figure perched on a bald spot on the enormous weathered tree stump that had been dropped at the tree-line by an especially-intense storm several years ago. The short trunk of the old-growth fir was too tall to climb, so the only way to the top was to scale the exposed tentacles of the huge root ball tipped on its side.

The white baseball cap told her it was Willie Moses, who she hadn't seen since Junior had been killed. Funny how troubled kids craved height, she thought, thinking back to her own childhood. Usually, Willie was sitting staring out to sea from the highest point of the stump when she saw him but today, he was standing, watching her approach.

He raised his arm in greeting, as was his custom, but immediately started his descent down from his perch. Willie always waited patiently for her to climb up to his spot, never presuming she wished his company. But today he was on the sand waiting for her by the time she reached the stump. Alarmed at first, Baylou quickly realized she should have expected it.

"Where's Junior?" he said, his voice touched with concern, even before she could ask why he wasn't in school. They had always spent their time together atop the big stump while Junior waited below, although Willie would always climb down to spend several minutes stroking the big dog's head before they departed.

"Something got him, gutted him in the night," she replied, shaking her head. "Before Christmas."

"Wolf," Baylou added. "Saw the tracks. Big one. Heard lots of howling too. More than one out there. New pack, I think."

"Oh," Willie said in his characteristically subdued voice, looking down.

After a moment of silence, he looked up at her and added sadly, "Another one."

"Another one what?" asked Baylou, concern in her voice.

"Dead dog. Three last week at Opitsat. More before that, I think. Heard Uncle Jack tell my dad. I was supposed to be in bed but I sat in the hall."

"What did he say, Willie?" she asked.

"Not sure. Wolves cornered kids on the beach, it sounded like. Tried to pull them into the forest. But their dad and uncle chased them off. I think he said one of the kids got bit bad, on the leg, maybe? Other one had the leg of his jeans ripped off, or that's what it sounded like."

"And?"

"Well, I'm not sure exactly, but it sounded like Uncle Jack made a big deal out of telling everyone to keep quiet, said he'd fix it. And not to take the kid that got bit to the hospital. I think he's still pissed about that incident with his grandson and the way the Mounties backed up the doctors, you know about that. I told you, didn't I? Anyway, Nurse Irene gave the kid stitches, said he'll be OK."

"Scary!" commented Baylou in a low voice.

"Yeah, people are spooked. I think Uncle Jack said something about lots of howling over the last few weeks. And maybe something about some wolves on the beach in broad daylight that isn't normal, something like that."

"What else?" Baylou asked, fishing for details.

"Well, cattle are missing. Seems like no one's seen them for weeks. Oh, and something about someone out hunting saw a black bear carcass dragged out of its den by wolves and eaten. And something about a person being chased up the front steps of their house by a big white wolf. That's when Uncle Jack got riled up. He talked about it as if it was a ghost or something."

"Does Uncle Jack have a plan, or did he say?" Baylou prompted.

"Something about elders meeting tonight. Maybe some big fight going on, I couldn't understand all of it. Some folks want to let them be, others are scared. I missed some of it but I do remember Uncle Jack saying these wolves are different. Bold, aggressive, I think he said. And something about it being a really big pack, because of the howling. All kinks of odd howling, not being right."

He sat back then, which usually meant he was done talking. Baylou couldn't remember the last time Wille had had so much to say.

"Well, maybe Uncle Jack is right, these wolves probably came in from the mountains," she offered. "Most of them, anyway. It's snowed so much lately, upland wolves must be feeling pinched. Maybe they left to find food and less snow. More cold this winter, you know that, but I hear snowpack is way up, back in the mountains."

"For sure," replied Willie. "Heat going since way before Halloween at home. Doesn't matter, my bedroom's always cold. Nose is cold all the time. Mama says she can't remember this much cold."

"If a big pack is killing dogs and cows on the reserve, harassing folks, must be another pack killing around here," insisted Baylou. "This one's quieter. Soft howling, only sometimes. Once though, they really got going."

"Think I heard Papa say something about dogs at Tin-Wis going missing. This weekend," added Willie in a low voice. "Papa said he heard howling last night, didn't want me going to school or coming down to the beach today. But I snuck out. Papa was never afraid of wolves, before he talked to Uncle Jack."

He paused then added, "Me either, until you said about Junior."

"Listen to your dad, Willie," Baylou said with concern. "Go before dark. Leave sunset watching to the tourists. These aren't local wolves. Can't be trusted."

"Yeah, OK, I guess," Willie muttered. "You really think it's that bad?"

"Upland wolves don't know there's no deer here for them. Local wolves ate them all. Hard year anyway for local wolves, with the big litters last spring. No wonder bear numbers are down. Two big packs of upland wolves prowling, plus local wolves? Big trouble coming."

Chapter 14

Friday 5 January 4:00 pm

In the waning light of dusk, two young men scrambled down a narrow trail from the wooded tombolo at the north end of Chesterman Bay and splashed through a few inches of incoming tide onto Mackenzie Beach. They'd been hiding out on the forested hill overlooking the beach for the last couple hours, pretending to enjoy the ocean view and upcoming sunset while steeling their nerve for the last part of their journey. Although they'd have preferred to wait until dark to move on, the incoming tide had forced their hand: their refuge was fast becoming an island and would remain so until the tide went out again.

However, it had started to pour rain and the gloom had driven all but the most dedicated beach walkers away.

Nineteen-year-old Sam, who'd led the decent down the trail, shifted his large backpack into a more comfortable position small frame and headed north along the water's edge. His best friend Seth had slipped on the muddy trail and had to run to catch up.

"Are you sure this is going to work?" twenty-year old Seth asked breathlessly.

Sam turned and glared at him.

"Stop being such a nervous-Nelly! I told you ten times already! No one camps at the far end at this time of year. The manager checks the toilet at that end once a week, on Sunday night. We'll have at least six days, free and clear. No one will know we didn't go to your Aunt's cottage to study for exams, she'll think we're sick at home."

"What if your Dad notices the camping gear is missing?" Seth whined.

"Why would he, Seth? For crying out loud, there'd be absolutely no reason for him to go poking around in that end of the garage."

He both stopped talking as a pair of dog walkers headed the other direction waved a greeting. Both boys were slightly-built and were struggling with the large packs filled with camping gear but they didn't have far to go.

"I thought you wanted an adventure," Sam said after the walkers had continued down the beach. "Something meaningful to do instead of wasting time studying for exams we know we'll fail anyway."

"I do!" said Seth, emphatically. "I guess I'm just getting jumpy now that it's almost dark. What about bears?"

"They bear-proof everything around here," Sam assured him. "And I think bears hibernate in the winter anyway, so it shouldn't be a problem."

They had almost reached the north end of the beach and could just make out moving water ahead. Sam dug into his pocket for a small flashlight.

"All this water is coming from a stream that runs from the forest into the ocean here. The stairs should be right up there," said Sam, pointing towards the woods up ahead. "See that stairway, with the light at the bottom? There's another one hidden up ahead, nearer the stream. That's the one we want."

He shone a small beam of light along the top of the beach until he spotted a pile of rocks near the stream flow.

"There!"

"I don't see stairs," whispered Seth.

"It's more like wood and rock steps set into a trail, not stairs made of lumber, like the other one," answered Sam.

Sam forged ahead and clambered up the steep slope that was almost overgrown with bushes. He stopped to shine his light back and guide the way for Seth, who followed his lead. Twenty feet or so up from the beach, the trail widened as it ran alongside the stream and into the forest. They easily made their way up to the far end of a private campground.

"Wow," whispered Seth. "This is amazing!"

"I told you!" replied Sam. "The toilets are way up the road. If we tuck the tent in behind one of these trees, no one will even know we're here. And even if someone did see us, they'd assume we'd paid to camp here. Most people won't know the campsite's closed over the winter."

There was maybe a half dozen camp sites set into a cul-de-sac at the end of a gravel road. They decided on the one beside the stream closest to the beach trail because it offered the best option for keeping their tent out of sight from the road.

The next morning, the folly of their choice became apparent.

Seth had woken Sam up while it was still dark because he was afraid to make the trip to the toilet by himself. Cursing at his friend under his breath, Sam agreed to go with him, but only because he was secretly afraid to be left there by himself.

As they neared their campsite on the way back, it was just starting to lighten up enough to see the road without the flashlight.

Seth saw the first wolf up ahead and stopped abruptly, putting an arm out to grab Sam.

Sam saw it too and whipped his head around quickly to see another wolf standing silently behind them. Slowly glancing around, he noticed several sets of eyes watching them from the woods on their right.

The animals didn't make a sound. Then the wolf up ahead started to advance toward them. It didn't snarl or growl but its menacing stance and laid-back ears conveyed the full force of its intent. Sam glanced around to see the wolf behind them had also taken a few steps forward.

Seth broke first. He bolted toward the campsite nearest the beach but as soon as he moved the wolf out in front tackled him to the ground and grabbed at his coat. Sam watched his friend scream and kick at the attacking animal in stunned horror, until another wolf hit him from behind, knocking the wind out of him.

Sam twisted around and tried to get to his feet but the wolf grabbed his leg in a vise-like grip. As he cried out, another wolf was on him, pulling at his coat until it exposed his throat.

In short order, it was all over. Both boys fell silent as they bled from fatal neck wounds. The wolves dragged the bodies into the woods on the other side of the stream.

Chapter 15

Saturday 6 January 3:15 pm

Walking along the sandy shoreline north on Mackenzie Beach after lunch, Luke came up against the rocks that eventually became a cliff that curved seaward to form a wooded headland. He turned around to walk back.

He'd hoped he might run into Baylou scouring the beach after the morning high tide, so he stayed high up on the beach against the rocks, where the driftwood goodies she'd be after might be found lodged into crevices by the waves. There were a few shadowy breaks in the rock formations where the forest came down to meet the beach and he soon spotted her bike tucked in behind a huge drift log. Walking the other direction, he wouldn't have seen her but from this perspective it was clearly visible. He heard her before he saw her: she was up near the tree line, shouting into the trees.

"Devils!" she screamed. "No business. Just go!"

Several other walkers stopped and stared, then moved on, shaking their heads.

Luke sat on a log a short distance away. He looked, but couldn't see anything in the woods. He waited patiently for her to calm down and approached her when she finally turned away from the woods to reclaim her bike.

"Are they gone?" Luke asked her gently, hoping he didn't sound patronizing. He figured few people actually bothered to speak to her and hoped that being straight-forward might get her to open up.

"For now," she replied, matter-of-factly, after a few minutes, but without looking directly at him. "Getting too close, too bold. Going to be more trouble."

"More trouble? What have they done?"

"Murdered my dog. Killed Tin Wis dogs, Opitsat dogs, cattle too, probably. Who knows what else."

"What were you seeing there, in the trees?"

"Eyes."

"Who's eyes? What are they?"

"Wolves. What did you think? Fairies?"

"Wolves! Right here on the beach in the middle of the day?"

"Damn right. Too many. Not local, big trouble."

"I'm sorry to hear about your dog. He looked like a fine companion."

"In the night. Quiet. Stupid chickens slept right through."

"You said Tin Wis lost some dogs as well?"

"Willie said. Two dogs this weekend, one right off the beach. Disappeared, no trace."

"Who keeps cattle around here? I've never heard of Opitsat. Where is it?"

Baylou rolled her eyes in annoyance, as if this was the 10th time she'd been asked this question today.

"Opitsat First Nations reserve, across the water from here, Meares Island. Little village, not even 200 people. Almost see it from downtown. Only get there by boat or float plane. Missionaries brought cattle, early 1900s. Tried to turn Opitsat people into farmers. Hah! Fat chance. Cows went wild, learned to take care of themselves. Opitsat people are fishermen. Sometimes, they kill one to eat but mostly the cows just wander around the village, eat the seaweed off the beach. Freaks out tourists.

"Some years, wolves and cougars get a few. Now more than two dozen cows and half a dozen bulls. Big herd. Biggest herd in ages, really. Scrawny things. Willie said it's gone missing. Cattle hide in the forest sometimes, so maybe wolves got them, maybe not. No one knows. But dogs are missing over there too and people hear the howling. I hear howling. They're bold, these ones—watching, waiting. For weakness. Haven't bothered tourists yet, that would make the news."

"It sounds like you know wolves."

"Yeah, I do," she said, finally looking up into his eyes. "You're not from around here."

"My name's Luke Robinson," he said, reflexively moving to offer his hand but put it in his coat pocket instead. "I moved here a few months ago from Newfoundland. A few years ago, we had a large number of fatal attacks by hungry polar bears."

"Wolves ain't bears."

"Yes, I realize that, they're very different predators. But if wolves are putting people at risk, that concerns me. I live here now. What can you tell me about them?"

Baylou grabbed the handlebars and moved to mount her bike then seemed to change her mind. Instead, she pushed it forward along the hard-packed sand near the wash of the incoming waves and started to walk. Luke fell into step beside her, the fat-tired bike between them. He struggled to keep up with her in the loose sand but knew he didn't dare miss the invitation she had extended.

She started to talk in a low voice that just managed to rise above the sound of the surf.

"Upland wolves, these ones. Hungry. Hard winter for them, lots of snow. First really bad winter in a long time, more than fifty years maybe. Good years mean plenty of deer and elk for them, so lots of pups survive. More packs roam the hills, looking for food.

"Small packs live around here now, mostly in the Park. Not much food for them. None here when I first came. Last year more pups survived. Some say mating with dogs but I don't think so. Hard to tell. I don't know but some say hybrids are less shy but just as strong, so more deadly when times are tough.

"New pack lives out of the Tonquin forest, above town. Small pack, bigger now. Come down here to the beach sometimes. No one sees them. Eat raccoons and bear cubs, deer if they can find them, dogs running loose, stuff the tide brings in overnight.

"Last few weeks are different. Weird quiet howling sometimes. From all directions. Pack talk. Three packs, I think, maybe more. Here and my side too, coming from the east, across the Mud Flats.

"I know folks hear the howling. hear them talking, gossiping. All gushy, feeling special about themselves to have wolves around, nonsense talk. Like some gift from nature, just for them!

"Stupid! Wolves get hungry enough, they eat anything. Dogs first, easy. Defenseless, really. Warn them off or next they go for the kids. You never want them feeling it's OK to go for the kids, you have a big problem. You got to let them know they can't be killing your people.

"Wolves are shy. They like elk and deer. Eat geese, raccoons, black bears—even beaver. Not people. But when they get really hungry, they figure out people are defenseless. Then they take down a human same as a deer. Kids first, they're easier, smaller."

"How do you know all this?" Luke finally interjected.

"I'm not stupid! Folks think I'm crazy, I hear the talk. Don't bother me. I know things, done things. No wolves here at first, all hunted out. But I had trouble with a pack after I moved to my cabin. Lots of snow that year. Watched me, those wolves did. Watched me hiking on the trails and even on my own porch. Lost all my chickens, no way to keep them safe. No gun then, no money.

"All these years, I walk the woods, listen, pay attention to howling. Talk to people who've lived here forever.

Willie's folks know wolves, about the hybrids. How to live with them, respect them, protect against them when you need to. They know when wolves are having trouble. They know wolves eat their dogs, always have done. Not all their people agree. Most understand life is tough for animals sometimes, just like for people.

"I knew cousins of Willie's grandfather, they talked to me. Not to people in town, the tourists, the cops—how to really live with wolves. Tourists and town folk think wolves do no wrong. Stupid people.

"Willie's people taught me. Wolves have powerful spirits and mostly, that's good. But things get tough in their world, they protect themselves. Mating with dogs, eating dogs, packs banding together to hunt. Do what they have to do. When times are tough for wolves, you have to stand up for your people."

"What should we do now?" asked Luke gently, almost afraid to speak, in case it broke her talking streak.

"Stand up to them. Stand up for your people. Don't turn your back. Don't run. Don't ever run."

"And if they attack?"

"You kill them. You don't, they kill you. More than one, that's big trouble, they get you. One person can't fight a pack. Tourists don't want to hear that, town folk don't want to hear that, Parks even more so. Trouble coming with that. Soon."

"How soon? Can you tell?"

"A week, maybe. Days, maybe. Might be too late. So much goes on in the dark. So many secrets. Something will set them off. Then it will explode."

Luke couldn't tell if she meant the wolves or the people.

"How will we know when we've reached that tipping point?"

Baylou stopped and scowled at him as if he were daft.

She shook her head in something like impatience or disgust—maybe both—but finally responded.

"When people start to die," she said calmly, staring at him intently.

Then she turned away from him, gave the bike a quick push forward to get going and rode off down the beach.

Luke stood in the sand watching as she headed toward the distant rocky point, where he knew there was another road access. Suddenly she stopped, put one foot on the wet sand and turned around to face him.

"I'm Baylou," she shouted, just loud enough for him to hear.

He nodded his head in reply and lifted his hand in a wave. He thought he detected a slight nod as she turned and resumed riding.

Chapter 16

Saturday 6 January 4:00 pm

Baylou thought about her encounter with Luke as she rode home to her shack in the woods. It had been a long time since she had talked to anyone from town aside from Betsy. Quite simply, no one ever talked to her. She couldn't remember the last time she had talked to an attractive man. It must be decades.

Luke's tall and rugged good looks made her think back to her early days on the coast, when there were more men than women and she hadn't been without one for more than a few days. She could pick and choose among them, and she always chose tall and handsome, taller than her always felt best.

Luckily, her sixth-sense for the insecure buggers who tried to make themselves look better by belittling strong women kept her out of the worst kind of man-trouble.

She remembered it all like it was yesterday, a time-travelling capability that made the struggles of her day-to-day existence disappear for gloriously long moments while she rode.

The first, of course, had been Paul. She'd been at her most impetuous then, just after she'd left home.

Met him in Niagara Falls the summer of 1969. Smitten by his welcoming smile and soft hazel eyes, she'd let him buy her an ice cream cone. He said he was from New York, the city, so that's what she'd called him. As they ate, he talked, and with his words, painted for her such enticing pictures of long sandy beaches and gigantic waves on the Pacific coast that she couldn't resist.

Together, they'd headed back to Canada and then west across the country, sleeping and making love in the back of his old Rambler station wagon.

That was what she always remembered most when New York came to mind, that time they spent in the Rambler.

They'd bought a tent in Vancouver and took the ferry across to Vancouver Island. Once on the west coast, they joined the camp of squatters that had taken over Florencia Beach. But New York had left after a few weeks—wordlessly he'd packed up their tent the day after she'd said she wanted to stay at least another month and simply left without her.

She hadn't been worried. That night, she'd befriended the quiet, burly redhead with the outrageous sense of humour. He'd been on the beach almost a year, an American draft dodger, as New York had been, avoiding service in the Vietnam War. She could no longer remember where in the US he'd said he was from.

She happily moved into the huge driftwood and tarpaulin shelter he'd built into a nook along the treeline. Well beyond the reach of the waves, the hut was equipped with a crude wood stove cobbled together from a scavenged oil drum and discarded kerosene cans wired together for a flue. With heat and enough space for at least a dozen visitors, the place was in perpetual party mode.

That was when she'd taken on her name, leaving behind the label imposed on her at birth. He was Blaze, she was Baylou. No last names to pin them down.

Blaze at her hip, she'd flourished in the new lifestyle. Blaze explained how to set up an account to sell her wood carvings at the art shop in Ucluelet. Whatever cash she made bought food for the both of them.

Sometimes, she had enough to buy a tube or two of paint, which she used to embellish the drift wood on the inside and outside of the shack. She saw the creation of these images as the first grownup step in her childhood dream of becoming a professional artist—the carvings she dismissed as trinkets only tourists would buy.

She was loyal to Blaze for more than two years until he left without warning. She never did find out what had happened to him. He simply disappeared late one night with some guy who'd turned up a few weeks before in an old, oddly-pink Studebaker. Since disappearing hadn't been unusual for the two of them, she hadn't fretted over it when she noticed they were gone. She simply assumed they'd be back in a few days.

But they never did return.

She stayed alone in Blaze's shelter for a week until the Parks people suddenly swooped in and ran them all off the beach. That was the fall of '71 and she wondered if

Blaze had known the eviction was about to happen and hadn't told her.

The next 15 years or so after she'd moved to Tofino were a bit of a blur and her memory always glossed over that time, avoiding the painfulness of struggling to keep a roof over her head and making enough money for food.

On this day she felt brave enough to admit there'd been quite a parade of men in her life during that time. She knew she'd been the core of a small community living the same lifestyle. She couldn't remember any of those men any more, although a vague recollection surfaced of at least one bad experience. She again blamed herself for getting so stoned that she let down her guard and was proud she'd successfully resolved to be more careful.

Then came Ziggy, which always made her smile. She'd met him a few days after moving into Poole's Land in the late '80s. He'd been even taller than she was and more broad-shouldered but just as strong in spirit. They became fast friend and lovers soon after.

Ziggy had tightly-curled yellow-blonde hair that fell beyond his shoulders and a thick blonde beard tinged with red. His tropical blue eyes were as striking as hers and his skin took on the same honey-brown tan. They were so alike they could have been fraternal twins and that's what the group called them, 'The Twins.'

They'd been together for more than four years when Mingo came to Poole's. She smiled even more broadly at the thought of Mingo and her eyes lit up. That Luke fellow reminded her of Mingo.

In looks, Mingo was almost the polar opposite of Ziggy, except for his height. He was tall and wiry, with the wavy black hair, deeply tanned skin, and royal blue eyes of his Spanish heritage. He kept his beard short and his hair shoulder-length.

She remembered with a smile how he'd comb the thick mass of hair with his fingers to get it off his face when he talked in earnest.

For reasons she could not have explained—and she'd thought about it a lot—she and Mingo had gravitated to each other almost instantly. Within a week, the day after he'd touched her hand and she'd felt that jolt of his energy run through her, she had moved into Mingo's tent, leaving the rough-built shack she had shared with Ziggy for so many years.

Ziggy seemed to feel no animosity. He'd told her he could see how attracted they were to each other, even he could feel the electricity between them.

It had surprised her that passion so equally intense could play out so differently. Being with Ziggy had been comforting, his quiet strength had drawn her to him immediately and their lovemaking had been emotionally powerful. After four years with him, she had felt settled, calm, and confident to an extent she had never experienced before. She had taken up painting again, although drift wood and scrap boards were the only canvases she could afford.

Mingo's sinewy strength, on the other hand, was like nothing she had experienced before. She'd felt it the first time he'd touched her. It had come with a fierceness that elevated sex with him to an animal level, which had been a little scary. Sex with Mingo had been oddly addictive and definitely energizing.

Definitely not comfortable, she mused, shaking her head even now at the thought.

He had also not been one to sit around doing nothing all day and suddenly, neither was she. He was fired up about protecting the old growth forest and insisted they join the protest camp at Kennedy Lake that spring. She hadn't objected. Suddenly, being part of something bigger than herself was something she felt as passionate about as she did about him.

Mingo had been the last of the men in her life. It was always him her thoughts turned to as she thought of her life.

It was because of Mingo that she now had a home of her own.

It turned out that a secure place to live was all she had needed to become the artist she had always dreamed of being. In her time-travelling, she always tried to focus on everything he had given her, not what she had lost.

Even what she had lost was a blessing for which she was eternally grateful, and such final thoughts always left her feeling at peace.

Wolf Packs on the Move

In another place, at another time...

October on the west coast of Vancouver Island in 2028 had been incredibly unsettled—storms with horrific wind and torrential rain, one after another. Snow came by the middle of November to the western beaches. December had brought even colder temperatures and record-breaking snowfalls to the coast, which continued into January.

But up in the mountain valleys, especially those surrounding the high peaks of Strathcona Provincial Park, the cold had brought blizzard after blizzard. Now the snow was piled up thicker on the ground than it had been in living memory. But in Clayoquot Sound, logging activity had continued throughout the epic winter.

On the late afternoon of the 12th of January, almost due east of Tofino, the driver of a big log carrier barreled his rig down a snow-covered gravel road toward a new logging site, the empty trailer bouncing crazily when the wheels hit a deep rut. The company he worked for had a permit to selectively log deep into the northwestern section of the Taylor River drainage about five miles from the Strathcona boundary, near the western end of Great Central Lake. The small crew he was a part of was hauling the last of the stored logs from last season into the mill at Port Alberni over the winter; the work of falling trees would pick up after the snow had cleared.

The rough road ran through thick, virgin rain forest and the atmosphere was decidedly gloomy. Low clouds obscured the tree tops all day and snow was piled high on both sides of the road. A grader had been through since the last snowfall. There was a tricky section up ahead with several sharp turns. Driver Ned Komar took it as fast as he dared, not wanting to lose control of the trailer around the curves.

As he did so, he remembered something that had happened right here more than a month ago now, weeks before Christmas, which he'd meant to pass along to his boss.

That time, he'd been empty as he was today, and had been picking up speed as he came out of that last corner, knowing there was a straight stretch ahead. But he'd seen something on the road up ahead that made him hit the brakes.

It was a large pack of wolves—easily the largest he'd ever seen. More than two dozen animals, he thought, at least two of them jet-black. The wolves had stopped to stare at the truck but soon began scrambling over the snow berm on the left shoulder to get off the road.

Deer and bears often used the logging roads as trails, so you always had to be alert. Coming around a corner to find the road filled with wildlife was always a nasty surprise. All too often the encounter ended in carnage.

That time, all the wolves made it out of the way easily. He'd slowed to a full stop, peering intently into the woods as the dark forms slipped into the woods. The last one in line, who stood out almost pure white against the dark trees, stopped and looked back at him long enough to send chills down his spine.

Then they were gone. He sat staring at the point in the forest where they had disappeared for a good 10 minutes, as if he couldn't quite believe what he had seen.

As if coming out of a trance, he had engaged the parking brake and grabbed his gloves and tire iron from the passenger seat of the cab. He opened the door and eased down out of the truck. As he pulled on the gloves, he eyed the patch of trees where the wolves had once been.

Satisfied they were gone he walked ahead of his truck to inspect the tracks in the snow. He could see where the pack had crossed the snow berm on the right side of the road where a narrow game trail in the snow snaked out of the trees. Then they had mingled in the middle of the road, their tracks crisscrossing every which way in the compressed snow. The tracks then went over the snow berm on the left and into the woods.

There were no marks in the road ahead of the area of crisscrossed tracks and that had confused him in a way he hadn't quite understood until he walked to the back of the truck and continued for a minute or so along the road behind it. There were the tracks from his truck and nothing else.

The wolves hadn't been using the road to travel on, as most animals did. They were simply moving across it on their way to someplace else. He turned and stared again at the place where the pack had disappeared into the forest, wondering where they were headed to with such purpose.

After a few moments, he'd given his head a shake and returned to the truck. As he released the brakes and put the rig into gear, he'd made a mental note to tell the crew chief about the wolves. But when he'd got into camp, there'd been a ruckus over a log-picker that had landed in a gully and it had slipped his mind. A few days later he was out for his Christmas break and the opportunity was gone.

The company was supposed to inform the government conservation office about all wildlife sightings, especially cougars and wolves. Nearby Strathcona Park had abundant deer and elk that were preyed upon by cougars and wolves. The elk seemed to stay inside the park boundary where they belonged; as far as he knew, no one had even seen them here on the logging road. However, deer were common all year round, bears in the summer and fall. In the last two years, he'd seen wolves maybe twice and one of the other drivers had once seen a cougar.

But a wolf pack as large as the one he had seen was a real novelty. As the rig picked up speed, he made himself another mental note to tell the boss.

When he pulled into camp an hour later, he headed first thing to the crew chief's trailer and saw the boss coming out the door.

"Donovan!" Ned called out. "Just the man I need to see."

"What is it? Something wrong?"

"No, no, I just remembered something on the trip in, about a wildlife sighting I forgot to report last month. A huge pack of wolves that passed over the road near the creek at Milepost 73, at the beginning of December, on the 1st I think, a Friday. More than two dozen, including one big white one. It was odd, though. They were clearly just crossing the road, heading southwest towards Clayoquot Sound."

"You're sure?"

"Yeah, I got out of the truck once they were gone and checked the tracks. They hadn't been traveling the road, they were crossing it. If I hadn't come along right then, I would have missed them."

"Interesting. You know, Henley was the last to leave before Christmas and told me that on his last run he'd stopped to inspect some churned up snow on the road at Mile 27. He claimed it was a whole bunch of mixed-up wolf tracks that didn't go up or down the road, just down over the berm on the east side and up-and-over on the west. He never saw any wolves but he thought he counted more than a dozen individual tracks. That would have been at least a week after your sighting. Doesn't seem like it could have been the same pack. He didn't take any pictures or anything, so it didn't seem like something worth reporting. But now I'm thinking maybe it was."

"Two big wolf packs within a week, both heading west? That seems a little odd," replied Ned.

"Yeah, it does, doesn't it?" said Donovan. "It's probably the deep snow driving them out of the mountains, looking for food further west. Come with me and we'll get the details down so I can include it in my January report. Conservation folks will probably want to document this information."

Chapter 17

As he strolled along the water line at Mackenzie Beach, Luke thought about his encounter with Baylou last week and his discussion about it with Blake last night.

While sharing a few beers—at *his* kitchen table for a change—he'd tried to explain to Blake why he was concerned.

"I hate to admit it, but her prophesy that there's trouble coming from the wolves around here has me worried," he said, shaking his head. "I've never had to deal with wolves before. I've never heard of anyone having problems with them in the Arctic. My understanding is that wolves rarely, if ever, attack people. But Baylou seemed convinced the wolves around here have become an imminent threat."

"But did she really give you a valid reason for why she felt that way? It seems to me it's all just a feeling she has that isn't supported by any solid evidence."

"Well, a wolf did kill her dog and probably several others. And maybe cattle as well. That does seem to support the conclusion that they're having trouble finding food."

"That's been true around here for quite a while though, as far as I know. Off and on, dogs have been attacked by wolves on the beach. There was one the year before I got here that folks were still talking about. But as far as I know, there's never been an attack on a person."

"There's always a first time for anything, though—you know that," replied Luke.

"Yeah, OK, but the information pamphlet that Parks Canada hands out says the problem comes from people being irresponsible with their dogs," she retorted.

"Maybe, but Baylou seems to think some of these wolves aren't local," he pointed out.

"OK, even if that's true—based on what, exactly?— how much difference would that make?"

"I guess the pattern of howling is all she's going on, coupled with the weather," he finally admitted. "And it could be that some of these outsiders aren't truly wild wolves but packs of hybrids."

"Why does it matter?" Blake asked.

"I'm not sure," he acknowledged with a sigh.

Blake had just shrugged and looked at him with raised eyebrows. It was too inconclusive. He needed more information.

So, he'd taken to walking along the beach for the last few mornings, hoping he might run into Baylou again and see if he could get more details from her about her premonition.

Today, he lucked out.

Up ahead, he saw her up by the giant tree stump, balancing her bike and talking to a kid who looked about 10 years old wearing a white baseball cap. He wasn't sure he should interrupt but thought this kid might be her friend Willie, so he slowly walked towards them.

Baylou let him approach within a few feet, then promptly turned her back and started pushing her bike away. After going a few steps, she turned back and looked at Willie.

"He's OK," she proclaimed with a nod in Luke's direction. And then she headed off down the beach.

Mystified, Luke just stood there for a moment. Then he shrugged and turned back to the boy.

"Hi, I'm Luke. You must be Willie. Baylou told me about you."

"Yeah. You the photographer?"

"Yes, I am. But I also have some experience dealing with animal attacks and I've been wanting to ask Baylou more about the wolves. She seems to be a little bit shaken up by the death of her dog," Luke offered.

"Yeah, I really liked him. Not like our dogs. He'd sit with me," Willie responded in a quiet voice.

"You must miss him too," Luke said sympathetically.

"Yeah."

"I had a dog when I was your age," added Luke. "He wasn't a cuddler but he was good companion. I used to take him hunting and he was great to have around."

"You hunt?" Willie asked, his youthful voice tinged with disbelief.

"Yes, when I get a chance. That doesn't happen so often now but I hunted a lot when I was in high school. It was my favourite thing to do."

"Me too!" Willie replied. "Dad took me when I was little. Go with my uncles now. Deer and elk. Sometimes bear."

"You hunt bear? That's impressive," Luke said with respect. "I used to live in the Arctic and I've had to kill a few polar bears in my time."

"Yeah?"

"They can be really scary," offered Luke. "The males are enormous. And fast—boy, are they fast. Hard to believe an animal that big can be so fast."

"Black bears are fast too," Willie objected. "And wolves. Why you don't run. They'll get you."

"Very true," Luke admitted. "Humans are awfully slow."

He noticed the boy fidgeting now, which he hadn't been doing earlier. He wondered if just talking to him was starting to make the boy uncomfortable.

"I guess I'd better get on with my walk," Luke said. "See you around?"

"Sure," Willie responded with a wave.

Chapter 18

Thursday 11 January 2:35 pm

Luke had given up trying to way-lay Baylou on the beach again with the hope of getting any more information out of her and decided to look elsewhere.

After spending several hours phoning around the wildlife experts and industry informants he knew to find out more about wolves on the west coast, he finally found a retired provincial conservation officer named Rex Matterson willing to talk to him.

"Don't quote me on any of this, but you should know the trouble with wolves out there has been going on for decades," he said. "The locals like to blame tourists anytime there's a spike in attacks on dogs but in my opinion the problem's more complicated and long-standing than that."

"How so?" asked Luke. "I admit I know very little about problems with wolves. Even hunting in northern Alberta when I was a kid, I remember them being more shy than black bears. You hardly ever saw them but sometimes heard them howling. And there were even fewer issues with them up in the Arctic."

"Yeah, I know," responded Rex. "But the situation on Vancouver Island is different. First off, virtually all wolves on the island were killed off by the mid-20th century. Which means that when the Pacific Rim park opened in 1971, there were no wolves left and likely hadn't been any around for at least 20 years. It's impossible to know how many there were before that, but based on the number of animals deliberately killed up until the early 1960s, including those taken by bounty hunters and those trapped and sold for pelts, they were probably fairly common.

"However, with numbers driven so artificially low after they were hunted out, we know there was some hybridization going on with dogs that had run wild. That introduced the genes for black coat colour into the population: domestic dogs often have it, wild wolves never do—which means you don't get black wolves unless you've got some inter-species hanky-panky going on."

"I've never knew that," admitted Luke.

"It's a small thing, but important—kind of a marker for hybridization, no matter how long ago it happened. To understand the rest, you have to look at a map," Rex continued.

"In the early 1970s, wolves started moving over from the central B.C. coast onto northern Vancouver Island between Port McNeill and Campell River—by swimming between the cluster of smaller islands that link that area of the big island's northeast coast to the mainland. Island-hopping, we call it.

"Those wolves did very well and spread quickly beyond that region in the 1980s. By the late 1990s, they'd heavily colonized almost the entire west coast and the huge wilderness areas in and around Strathcona Park in the middle of the island. Lots of elk live up in that northern interior as well as deer. Perfect wolf habitat meant they successfully raising litter after litter of pups.

"They did so well it put them into competition with cougars, who'd come to rule the north island and the west coast. But because wolves working in packs can successfully kill more prey than cougars hunting as individuals, in short order the wolves pushed most of the cougars out of the west coast as far south as Port Renfrew. Now, generally speaking, cougars dominate the entire east coast down to Victoria, while wolves rule in the north island, in Strathcona Park, and along the west coast. There are still cougars on the west coast and wolves near Victoria, but not nearly as many as there used to be.

"We actually saw the result of this semi-replacement of cougars with wolves reflected in the early 21st century history of wildlife encounters. Hikers and residents on the west coast all of a sudden were having less issues with cougars and more incidents involving wolves. The wolves became accustomed to meeting people on the hiking trails and beaches—and got bolder and bolder. Several farms just north of Port Alberni, which is in the direct path of newly-formed packs leaking out of Strathcona Park to the north, had problems with wolves killing and harassing livestock and threatening people between 1999 and 2007—so much so that the packs had to be eliminated. The media never found out about those incidents or decided not to report them. But conservation people knew.

"Why wouldn't the media report on wolf attacks?" asked Luke.

"You're underestimating the power of the prevailing narrative that says wolves are not a threat to people," Rex replied. "Since the 1970s especially, people have been conditioned to believe that wolves and people coexisted harmoniously for thousands of years in North America before Europeans arrived. Conservationists successfully convinced virtually everyone that the wholesale slaughter of wolves in the 18th and 19th centuries was driven by a baseless fear of wolves instilled in European colonists by fairy tails."

"Yes, I've certainly understood that to be true, from people I've spoken to and articles I've read," replied Luke.

"Well, the problem is that most conservationists these days, including many university-trained biologists, consider it their job to act as bulldog activists, which means they go after any reporters, journalists, or news outlets that dare suggest wolves are capable of attacking and killing humans—or even that wolves can become a serious problem for farmers and ranchers. So the media have learned to keep a low profile on these issues and conservation folks who aren't comfortable being activists simply keep their mouths shut. For the same reason, members of the public are also reluctant to report frightening encounters they have with wolves. That means we never really get to know the true extent of the problem."

"I've sometimes run into that phenomenon with polar bears, but I never realized it might be even worse for wolves," said Luke.

"I think that's because there's more wolf interactions with people, both across North America and in Europe," replied Rex. "And now that wolf numbers have recovered over most of their range, conflicts have naturally increased."

"I'm surprised there hasn't been an attack by a wolf, or wolf pack, on a person out on the west coast of the island, to be honest," he said continued soberly. "Wolves are naturally shy and don't generally let you see them, so when they do, it's deliberate—they're not trying to make friends, as people often assume—they're testing whether you'll be suitable prey. If you don't scare them off when they first make themselves seen, they keep coming closer and closer to see how dangerous you might be, until they finally attack."

"I didn't know that about wolves," admitted Luke.

"Most people don't," replied Rex. "But it's becoming increasingly obvious that this behaviour is how wolves deal with their first encounters with people. And given how acclimated these Tofino area wolves are to having people around and how tenuous their food supply is, all it would take would be a poor year for natural prey or a year when they've simply eaten up all the natural prey in the area, for them to turn from attacking dogs to attacking humans. Just like that attack in northern Saskatchewan years back."

"I remember that one," Luke replied. "Young man killed and eaten by several wolves not far from a mining camp. Some biologists insisted it was a bear."

"That's the one. As I said, there's a still a powerful belief that healthy wolves won't go after people or livestock. In fact, the early Europeans that came to North America knew better. It's why they killed them all off. European and Russian fairy tales were likely based on real experiences, written to teach children to be afraid of wolves.

"Most people also don't know that Russia still has an enormous population of wolves that cause them trouble every few years or so. They've even had the formation of huge superpacks in Siberia—one involving about 400 animals—which only seem to happen when shortages of natural foods cause packs to coalesce to hunt anything in their path. We've never seen that here in North America to that degree, as far as I know. We might see dozens rather than hundreds of animals coming together. But it's clear that superpacks can develop anywhere under the right circumstances."

"Wow. That's a scary thought," Luke replied with astonishment. "And do you think there's anything to the idea I heard from one resident that there are packs moving west into the Tofino area from the interior of the island, because of the snow in the mountains? Would they do that?"

"Oh, yes, absolutely," replied Rex. "We know they've moved west because of winter snow before—in fact, it may be why they ended up colonizing the west coast in the first place, moving out of Strathcona Park because of winter snow. But as far as I know, in recent years they've never moved all the way into the Tofino area proper. They usually stop as soon as they find enough food, but they might keep going if the circumstances were right."

"OK, but what about the hybrid issue?" Luke asked. "Does the fact that Vancouver Island wolves have dog genes make them more dangerous—or less?"

"If you think about it a little, you'll have the answer yourself. In general, most first generation wolf-dog hybrids are less wary of humans than wild wolves are, and harder to scare off. That's because the dog part of them is so much less aggressive and more curious. But a hybrid can be just as big as a wild wolf, as cunning, and just as strong. These traits automatically makes a first-generation hybrid more dangerous. But the truth is, we know very little about what happens to that dog-like behaviour when those hybrids breed back into wolves over more generations."

"That said, entirely wild wolf packs that have gotten used to people being around and are also food-stressed, can also cause a lot of trouble. Those packs attacking livestock and people outside Port Alberni were pure wild wolves, as was the pack that killed that man in Saskatchewan. And we're sure now that the wolves that have attacked dogs at Long Beach on the west coast over the last few decades were pure essentially wild wolves, not recent hybrids."

"So, let me see if I've got this straight. A first-generation hybrid can be as big as a wolf, so the only definitive difference if you're looking at a wolf in the wild is that a pure black wolf must be a hybrid," said Luke.

"Well, not quite, because that black gene can be from a hybridization event that happened 40 years ago or only two years ago. And I've been told there are also slight differences in the way wolves and hybrids move because a first-generation hybrid usually has a wider chest that comes from its dog heritage, which also means their tracks are slightly different. But it takes a really experienced tracker to tell them apart. With dead animals, there are some skull shape differences in first generation hybrids, and DNA tests are reasonably accurate up to about three generations back. But DNA tests usually take weeks to get results back, so they're often not helpful in a crisis."

"Just great!" sighed Luke in frustration. "So we won't really know if the animals causing trouble here are recent hybrids or not until all the damage is done. That's a problem because I get the distinct impression that many people would be alright killing problem animals if they're hybrids rather than wild wolves."

"Yeah, that's probably true," replied Rex. "But as I said, we have no evidence that hybrids were involved in recent attacks elsewhere, so it's unlikely to be the case here. We keep going back to the fact that people have been told repeatedly that wolves very rarely attack people because it's just not in their nature, when that isn't always true.

"And remember that these particular wolves have only been living on the west coast for 30 years or so—these are not the same animals that co-existed with First Nations people in this region for thousands of years. These wolves are all relative newcomers to the area. They've had to learn to live in and around a very popular national park just as year-round tourism rates exploded. That's a lot more human activity than wolves usually have to deal with, which means these wolves are almost uniquely acclimated to people.

"It seems to me they may also be uniquely food-stressed much of the time, partly because they've already taken out most of the deer but also because having so many people around all the time just naturally restricts their hunting activities. You'll see people call them 'sea wolves' because they spend so much time on the beaches. But I think that a beach foraging strategy may be forced on these animals by the fact that they're such effective predators—that soon after these packs moved onto the coast, they drastically reduced local populations of forest prey like deer and beaver."

"I never thought of it that way before," replied Luke. "Is that why the pictures of wolves around Tofino I've seen always show quite skinny animals?"

"I'd say so, yes," Rex responded. "Wolves have managed to exist in areas like Tofino by picking off some of the raccoons and bears that thrive where people settle, as well as any naïve deer that move in from outside. They certainly do eat spawning salmon in the fall in other regions, but as far as I know, there are no functioning salmon streams around Tofino. Most of the time, the coastal wolves in your area are reduced to scavenging anything edible they can find on the beach. They may be able to take the odd seal or otter if they're lucky but really, I'd say it's no wonder that sometimes hunger drives them to kill and eat dogs."

"It's attacks on dogs I've heard most about," Luke admitted. "Those seem to be happening more often than even a year ago. People are telling me that dogs running loose on local beaches, and on the First Nations' reserves, are just disappearing without a trace. But there have also some very threatening encounters with people that only by luck didn't end in disaster."

"Makes perfect sense to me," Rex replied without hesitation. "And I'll add that although I've never heard anyone say so publicly, I think that for a long time now, Parks Canada has not been entirely truthful about the extent of trouble they've been having with wolves. I also suspect at least some First Nations may be getting concerned by the reality of how these wolves are behaving.

"What do you mean by that?" asked Luke, genuinely puzzled.

"Well, we hear a lot about their traditional stories describing their close relationship with wolves. But the reality is that few aboriginals alive today actually *knows* what living with wolves day-to-day in this landscape was really like before European attitudes to wolves became dominant. Before these mainland wolves arrived, there was a period of 50 years or more when there were virtually no wolves around at all, and probably many decades before that when they were quite rare.

"But the public doesn't get that, and I'd guess many First Nations people don't either, especially the youngsters. Instead, they connect the stories told by elders about ancient wolves to the animals that live in the forest today, leaving out the fact that these are a completely different lineage of wolves than their ancestors knew. That worries me because the idealized notion that people can live in harmony with packs of wolves—but only if people adjust their behaviour to accommodate them—only works until wolves get the upper hand."

"I never thought of it that way," mused Luke. "I think I hear you saying that the pack structure of wolves might make a real difference in passing along knowledge of interactions with the people they know on the landscape. It's almost like they have a culture themselves, of sorts—

and because of that, the pack as a group can remember how their day-to-day relationship with a certain group of people should play out."

"Exactly!" Rex exploded. "I guess what I'm also getting at is that perhaps we aren't privy to *all* of the stories the indigenous elders have to tell. I just wonder if there aren't also cautionary tales from the old days that the elders haven't yet shared with anyone—stories about what to do when wolves refuse to live in harmony. I don't know if that's true but I think it's possible."

At this comment, Rex paused. Luke gazed out the window, his mind wandering to what Baylou had told him until Rex spoke again.

"But you know, Luke, once you have solid evidence to go on that there are wolf attacks on people actually happening, my recommendation would be to treat these packs as you would any habituated, misbehaving species of predator," Rex said confidently. "Ultimately, in terms of the conservation and protection of human life decisions that have to be made, that's all you can do ."

"Yeah, I guess you're right," sighed Luke.

"I wish you luck, Luke," Rex replied, concluding the call. "In all likelihood, it will all fizzle out as an issue after a few days, as it's done before. Sometimes these are just isolated incidents."

Chapter 19

Blake sat drinking her coffee as Luke launched into a rant about her boss's indifference to the information that wolves posed an imminent problem for the community, nodding occasionally in support. She didn't think she'd ever seen him this worked up.

"So, I took your advice and gave Sergeant Hammond a call. Told him what I'd heard from Baylou, from Betsy, and from Rex Matterson. He dismissed everything Baylou had to say as the mutterings of a lunatic, saying he hadn't heard anything from local First Nations about losing dogs or cattle, that people always exaggerate scary encounters with wildlife, and that Matterson's suggestion that wolf packs from the east would invade Tofino was ridiculous."

"Well, to be fair—as you've already told me—there have been wolf problems in the Park for a long time, well before Hammond got here," Blake replied. "The reports you've read suggest Park officials have things under control. If I'm understanding correctly what you've told me, these reports imply all wolf packs are based in the Park but sometimes range outside it, which gives them authority to dictate how people should behave both inside

131

and outside the actual boundaries of the Park. However, I don't think you've said how many packs operate on the entire peninsula, or if that's changed recently—probably because that information isn't being released by Parks officials."

"Yes, that's exactly right," Luke replied. "I feel like I'm simply not getting all the information that's available. If it's true that all the incidents worth mentioning in these reports have happened within the Park, why are there signs all over town warning folks about wolves? Is Baylou right that a pack has been living in the Tonquin Forest? Have there been encounters with wolves with locals on the Tonquin trails and elsewhere that aren't getting reported to the detachment—or to the media—because people assume these are park wolves?"

"I suppose it's possible," admitted Blake. "Perhaps the Mayor has been working with provincial conservation officers to deal with wolf incidents in town and they've left Hammond out of the loop."

"Or, as I've seen happen elsewhere, Hammond knows what's going on but has been advised to not make a big deal about it. After all, this entire town's economy is driven by tourist dollars and people who are frightened they might be facing a wolf attack aren't likely to visit," countered Luke.

"You could be right," admitted Blake. "I've always found him too much of a people-pleaser for my liking and if you ask me, that makes him vulnerable to political pressure."

"Well, there's also the possibility that Hammond's one of those people who've always believed that wolf attacks simply don't happen," Luke interjected. "It's something Rex mentioned and certainly I remember it coming up in relation to the Saskatchewan wolf attack years ago. There were all kinds of op-eds in the newspapers from both public officials and biologists insisting that wolves don't attack people, and that by default, it must have been a bear that killed the mine worker."

"Well, it *is* a common opinion," replied Blake, shrugging her shoulders. "Just about everyone I've ever talked to about the wolf warning signs, including locals and tourists, dismiss them as typical government scaremongering. They simply don't believe there's any real threat to their *own* safety and would honestly be thrilled to see a wolf pack. If they have any concerns at all, it's for their dogs. But even then, most of them won't go so far as to keep their dogs on a leash."

"Well, let's hope Hammond's right that the situation will resolve itself in a few days as it's done in the past—that Baylou and Willie's folks are right about what they're seeing and hearing but wrong about where it will lead."

Chapter 20

Friday 12 January 5:30 pm

In the week since Ian had left the Menagerie for his drafting work in Vancouver, the three left at the farm had heard wolves howling several times. The howling irritated Pete because the horses became skittish and hard to handle, and the donkeys brayed hysterically even if they were safe in the barn.

And after what had just happened, there was no keeping the news from Ian. So, when her husband called from Vancouver that night, Peg had to tell him.

"Yesterday, the wolves started calling before Jenny could get the goats into the barn for the night and the damn things refused to come down off the roof of the shed," Peg explained. "It took all three of us to get them to cooperate. Pete threatened to drive into Port Alberni for a gun then and there, insisting he couldn't wait for you to get back. But I managed to talk him out of it, and got him to agree to waiting a few more days at least."

"Then tonight, all hell broke loose," she said with some trepidation. "And I know you're not going to like it, but this time, there was an outside witness."

"What the hell happened?!" he demanded.

"It was a complete disaster," Jenny said, subdued at first and then louder as her emotions kicked in. "Pete and Jenny were in the horse barn getting the animals settled in for the night. I was feeding the chickens, waiting for Jenny to finish inside so she could help me coax the goats off the shed roof for the night.

"There'd been no howling at all day, no warning of any kind. The wolves just came out of the forest without making a sound. There were so many I couldn't count them from across the yard. One was completely white but all of the others were dark, some of them with light around the muzzle like you see in the newspapers. Two black ones immediately leapt onto the shed roof and each grabbed a goat by the throat. They ran off them as if they weighed nothing. Then more and more wolves came, like I said, I couldn't count how many."

"Oh my God," muttered Ian.

"Yeah. And once the goats realized they weren't safe on the roof, they started jumping down into the enclosure. But obviously, they weren't safe there either. Those that didn't get carried off into the forest had their throats slashed. They just lay in the yard twitching and gushing blood! The wolves disappeared through a hole in the electric fencing. Pete said for sure that hole wasn't there this morning.

"They broke through the fence?" asked Ian in disbelief.

"I guess they must have. Anyway, it was all over faster than you'd believe. I couldn't understand why Pete didn't come out and do something but he said the bawling of the

135

goats and my shouting made the horses bolt and rear-up before he could get them into their stalls. They were hysterical, running all over the place. He had to hide in one of stalls to get out of the way. Then he had to work his way around them to get to the barn door. That's why it took him so long to come out. But by then it was over. He didn't actually see anything of what happened."

"Damn it, he's supposed to be there to keep you safe too!" Ian exploded. "Not just the horses. It sounds like he was completely useless."

"It wasn't really his fault, Ian. We were all caught off-guard. Jenny was on the other side of the barn and had just gotten the donkeys in their stall when she'd heard me screaming and immediately tried to get to me. She saw the last half of the attack from the barn door. But she said she just couldn't understand what she was seeing, so she just stood there, watching. When Pete finally came out and realized what had happened, he counted only one goat left standing out of our entire herd. Seventeen goats dead or stolen! How is that even possible?"

"Our whole herd, just gone?" Ian groaned.

"I know, I know. It's horrible! But maybe the worst of it was that once I saw that Pete had come out of the barn, I started looking around. And I noticed someone standing on the road. It was that Baylou character we see riding her bike along the highway all the time."

"What on earth was she doing there?" bellowed Ian.

"I have no idea!" Peg replied in a shaky voice. "It really startled me to see her there. I don't think she's ever come on our property before. And it scared me, I didn't know why exactly, at first. Then I realized it made her a witness. All that effort to keep the attacks quiet blown to hell."

"Did she say anything to you?" asked Ian, his voice now more subdued.

"Not really—she just lifted her head and shouted "Bastards!" at the sky," replied Peg. "I couldn't tell if she meant us or the wolves. Then she just turned and wheeled her old bike down the drive without another word."

"Shit," whispered Ian.

"Please tell me what you want me to do, Ian," Peg begged. "I literally can't think straight right now."

"Just tell Pete and Jenny to clean up the mess and keep their mouths shut about it. Bury the dead goats that didn't get taken. We'll have to keep the place closed this weekend, of course, because someone will notice the goats are gone. I'm almost done here, so I'll get home as fast as I can. Just hang on, love, until I get there. Don't worry, it will all be OK."

Chapter 21

Friday 12 January 5:45 pm

Baylou muttered under her breath as she rode away from the carnage. What kind of morons decided to start a petting zoo and pony ride business in a forest filled with cougars and wolves? When this outfit had first moved in, she'd been sure the pony people wouldn't last a season. It surprised her that they were still here but she knew this wasn't the first trouble they'd had with killers from the woods.

She'd worried about cougars with all those animals since the day the goats had been delivered but more recently, wolves were a bigger concern. She'd surreptitiously kept an eye out for signs of an impending attack, especially after she'd realized a new pack must be in the area. Tonight, she'd had a bad feeling the wolves might move in big-time.

She didn't know the wolves had killed their pig a few days before but she knew they'd killed *something*. She hadn't wanted to worry Willie any more than he already was, so she hadn't said anything. But she'd started keeping track of the pattern of howling and expected more death tonight.

She'd been riding home along the bike path after buying groceries in town when she sensed the wolves nearby. A sudden quiet came over the other creatures in the forest, which put her instantly on alert. Most people never paid attention to these clues, they were simply oblivious to their surroundings.

She'd turned onto the road into the pony property to check and had arrived in the yard just in time to witness the assault from start to finish. She'd known the wolf pack was a large one but during the attack on the goats she thought she'd counted at least 20 animals. Could that possibly be right? She'd never known wolf packs around here to get that large.

She decided to peddle back into town and buy some beer. Doubling back would give the wolves time to eat and move on before she headed home through the woods. It would also give her time to let her anger dissipate. She knew she didn't think clearly when she was consumed by rage and she would need her wits about her now.

Baylou rode slowly along the bike path, letting her mind wander as she forced herself to relax and remember. She thought again about that tall handsome stranger she talked to on the beach, and how much he reminded her of Mingo.

Letting her thoughts run free, she remembered Mingo and the time of the protests, and how her life had changed so completely. Someone else might have found those thoughts disturbing but not Baylou. The memories grounded her and tonight, she let herself sink into them.

Her mind went back to the Kennedy Lake protest camp during the time everything around her had exploded. Thousands joined the local protesters and soon, the cops came. Many got arrested.

It had all kicked off on the heels of her realization, even without an official test, that she was definitely pregnant.

No one knew. Big shirts and ill-fitting men's jeans were standard fare for most of the girls. Mingo seemed clueless about her expanding waistline although in truth they'd spent little time alone together in those last few months. If he'd guessed, he never said.

She'd been almost 40 years old then and her shock lasted months. Mostly, she wondered how on earth it hadn't happened earlier. Stupidly, she hadn't ever given the idea of birth control much thought. Now, in the midst of the chaos, she was going to have Mingo's baby.

She wondered now, as she often did, if she'd have considered an abortion if she'd known early enough. Again, she decided the answer was no. Although that realization had sometimes puzzled her, she knew it was true. The thought of bringing a child into the world that was part Baylou and part Mingo had given her comfort as the baby inside her grew. Yes, and joy as well, even though she'd known, even then, that she had no ability to support a child.

In September, there'd been a nasty confrontation with the RCMP. A local couple who had their young child with them was on the verge of arrest for blocking the road. The cops were threatening to take their baby away

140

and both parents were frantic. Baylou caused a commotion on the other side of the road to distract the cops long enough for Steve and Amber to scurry with the baby to the safety of their van. Steve booted the van out of there so fast the cops didn't have time to react. They must have kept on driving east because she never saw them again.

But she'd gone a bit too far with her distraction and ended up arrested for her efforts. She probably shouldn't have bitten that cop or kicked the other one, she mused to herself.

She was taken to Port Alberni after the arrest and when they'd stripped her down, the guards realized how far gone she was. She was sent to another jail and later to a hospital when she went into labour. She gave birth to a tiny, gangly girl as dark as her father.

They would have to take the baby away, they said, for its own safety. She hadn't argued. She was going to jail. She'd heard Mingo had been arrested as well and sent somewhere else. Even *she* understood these were not places for a newborn.

When the social worker came to take the baby after only a few hours, she had had only one thing to say.

"I want her called Raven," she insisted, gently stroking the baby's thick dark hair with one finger. "It's important."

The social worker raised her eyebrows a bit but nodded. Baylou handed over the bundle, knowing she would never see her child again. For some reason, she was confident that the name she had bestowed upon her would see Raven through, protect her.

When she'd gotten out of jail several months later and returned to Poole's, Mingo's tent was gone and no one knew where he'd headed. Someone said he'd slipped out in the middle of the night. Ziggy was also gone but the couple who'd moved into his shack told her that Poole was holding something for her.

It turned out to be a big brown envelope that a lawyer had left for her. At first, she didn't want to open it but Poole said she was better off knowing than not.

She was utterly perplexed by the contents. In her wildest dreams, she could not have imagined what was inside. Indeed, she hadn't understood until Poole explained.

It was the deed to a 2-acre piece of property, "and all its amenities", transferred into her name by a Steven Wilson. There was a map showing the boundaries, which looked to be in the middle of nowhere off Sharp Road in Tofino, with no road access.

She still remembered scowling at the paper, trying to comprehend what it meant, and Poole gently explained that the man referred to in the document was the same 'Steve' that she had helped escape arrest. He and Amber had decided to leave the area entirely to keep their baby daughter safe but were so grateful to Baylou that they left her their almost-worthless piece of swampy property with its rough cabin.

And just like that, Baylou owned a place to stay for the rest of her life and a daughter who would carry a piece of her out into the world.

All because of a couple she'd barely known and a man she'd loved with all her heart. The thought, as always, made her smile.

She pulled into the one liquor outlet she still trusted and went in to buy beer. On the way home, she would think about what might be done about the wolves.

Chapter 22

Friday 12 January 7:30 pm

In town, Luke was standing at the till in the Co-op, mindlessly watching the cashier tally up the purchases moving past her on the conveyor belt and load them into a couple of tote bags. He turned at a slight commotion behind him and saw RCMP Sergeant Bob Hammond, in civilian clothes, abandon his grocery cart and bolt for the exit doors, cell phone to his ear.

"Something's up," Luke commented to the cashier in an off-hand manner, as a police cruiser shot past the window on its way from the detachment down the road, siren blaring and lights flashing. "Seems a little early for bar trouble."

"Not a fight," said the man behind him in line, his eyes on his phone. "Mounties found the body of Mitch Rodgers on the Tonquin Trail near the community centre. Looks like a bear got him."

Luke quickly paid for his purchases, shaking his head in wonder at how fast news travelled in a small town. It never ceased to amaze him. Cell phones had of course improved the efficiency but the information network of close-knit communities was always impressive.

When he reached his truck, he put his bags on the back seat and opened the driver's door. After a few seconds of thoughtful hesitation, he got in and headed towards the Tonquin trailhead, which was only a few blocks away. A fatal wildlife attack required a careful investigation. Even though he had moved across the country to get away from incidents like this and wasn't officially on duty, this town was his home now. He was still a wildlife safety specialist and should at least offer to help.

He drove rapidly up First Street, past the hospital. He took the turn left to the Community Centre and a few short blocks up the hill he saw a crowd had formed below the steps leading to the main entrance of the building. He pulled into the only parking spot that was still open on this level of the tiered parking lot and grabbed a flashlight out of the glove box. Avoiding the crowd, he noticed the officer trying to calm the people down was Blake. He left her to do her job and walked towards the prominent roofed sign that marked the trail down to the water.

There he saw Bob Hammond, now holding a rifle, huddled amongst a small group of men that included two of his constables, Cole and Eric, who both looked a little queasy.

Luke slowed his approach, not sure if his presence would be welcome. But as he entered the sphere of light around the men, Bob looked up and waved him in.

"Luke. I'm glad you came," said the sergeant in a low voice. "I'm sure we could use your take on this situation."

"What happened?" asked Luke, his eyes wandering to the prominent sign warning hikers to beware of wolves on the trail.

"We got a call about an hour ago from Mitch Rodgers' mother Allanna. He'd called her from the beach at about 5:00, saying he'd stayed late to paint the sunset but was heading back and would be home soon. When he wasn't home by 8:00 she called the detachment and asked if someone would have a quick look to see if his truck was still up at the parking lot, that it wasn't like him to not come straight home. She was worried he'd got hurt walking up the trail in the dark. Mitch is 18 but a small kid, quiet boy, likes to paint and draw the scenery; locals all know him.

"He'd left his truck here in the lot and it was still here with no sign of trouble, so my officers headed down the trail for a look. They had the quad, so it didn't take long. They found his body not far from here, near the junction of the main trail with the bike park, just before the bridge. He'd been dragged through the bush a ways and his clothes were all torn. His arms and legs are badly chewed. It looked as though he was ambushed by a bear as he walked past the bike park trail junction, so he may not have known what hit him."

"Were you able to get close enough to see if he was still alive?" asked Luke, looking at Cole.

"We really didn't want to get that close, to be honest. It didn't look like he could possibly still be alive and we could still hear the bear moving around in the bush. At one point our flashlight caught a glint of its eyes. It wasn't what we expected to find. It was really dark in there. We figured it would be safer to come back out and get reinforcements, more lights. And maybe a bigger gun."

"You actually saw a bear?" asked Luke, knowing most bears in the area should be hibernating. "Did you see any tracks?"

"We saw its eyes. And there was a powerful animal smell. The ground was too messed up to notice any tracks."

"OK, you did the right thing," Luke reassured Cole, patting his arm. "No sense risking getting attacked in the dark by an animal protecting its kill. At least now we have a general sense of what happened."

"Should we go back down and get him now or wait until morning?" asked Sergeant Hammon.

"We really need to go now," Luke replied. "This attack seems like a predatory kill, which means if we leave him, Mitch will be well and truly eaten by morning. I know that sounds gruesome but that's the reality of it. And if the bear is still there it needs to be dealt with before it attacks someone else. If we wait until it leaves the area, it will be that much harder to catch him and know we've got the right bear. If there's one awake right now, there could be others we don't know about.

"Bob, you'll first have to call the coroner and get permission to remove the body tonight. In my experience, if you agree to take lots of photos and make sketches of the scene, as you would do for a crime scene, they will usually agree. It will be a long night for everyone but this town is my home now and if my expertise is useful, I'm happy to help."

"OK, that sounds like a plan," said Hammond, looking around at the group. "We'll need several quads with trailers, a generator, and some big lights. I'll call the coroner and Cole, you ask Andrew to come out with his camera. I know it's late but we need him. And get somebody to open up the hall, we'll need it for bathroom breaks and food. Blake can be in charge of all that, serves her right for being the last one here."

Chapter 23

Saturday 13 January 8 am

After things had been settled at the Tonquin Trail head, Luke headed home. But he had trouble sleeping, and awoke tired and a bit irritable.

He put in a quick call to the detachment to see how Sergeant Hammond had coped with the follow-up on the attack.

"I got the coroner to agree to come," Hammond said with a sigh. "She was easily persuaded by the photos, as you suggested, but gave me a hard time about our conclusion that a bear was involved, given the time of year. She warned me to keep any theories like that to myself and to shut down any such speculation from my officers. I tried to tell her it was a bit late for that under the circumstances and she wasn't too pleased with me. I don't think she really understands what small towns are like."

"Did you get any rest last night at all?" Luke asked with sympathy.

"Not really," Hammond replied. "I understand her point about blaming the attack on a bear before we've analyzed all the evidence. But we get bears waking up during the winter all the time, especially big males. Even in relatively cold winters like this one. They just don't seem to go down as hard as females do, especially if they haven't had a chance to bulk up enough in the fall. And from what I understand, lots of things can rouse these bears from their sleep and set them off looking for food. I doubt this coroner's had experience with fatal animal attacks. Sounds like a city bureaucrat to me."

"Let's give her a chance," suggested Luke. "Discourage the bear-blaming as much as you can, just explain the evidence needs to be processed first. You won't be able to stop the rumours but you don't have to give them any fuel."

"Yeah, I can do that. But really, I don't think we'll see her coming to any other conclusion than that it was a big, hungry black bear. We've had close calls before and I don't see any reason to think this situation is going to be different."

Luke ended the call feeling unsettled and paced around the trailer. He'd had this kind of reaction from local law enforcement before and it never ceased to take him aback. Officers who wouldn't dream of jumping to conclusions about a human murder case before they had significant evidence seemed to lose their professional scepticism when marauding animals were involved.

That didn't bode well for this case, given he wasn't here in any official capacity. The whole thing could go side-ways really fast and there wouldn't be anything he could do about it.

**

After he'd hung up with Hammond, Luke walked down to the Gallery to check in with Betsy, who now felt like an old friend.

There he found the owner talking to a tall, dark-haired woman who was visibly upset but turned his way when he approached.

"This is Luke Robinson," said Betsy amicably.

"He's a special events photographer just moved here from Newfoundland," she added, as Luke offered his hand.

"Jenny Harris," she replied, taking his hand. "I work at the Marcus place, The Menagerie, helping out with the animals."

Luke couldn't help but notice that she was stunningly beautiful. She had a fine-featured face surrounded by long wavy hair that was even darker than his, as black and shiny as the local crows. Her eyes were a vibrant royal blue and she had strong, sinewy hands that contributed to a confident handshake, which Luke noticed immediately.

"The Menagerie? I've seen the sign but haven't had a chance to check it out. I've just moved here, only been in town a few weeks," Luke told her, moving a little closer.

"I'm relatively new myself," said Jenny.

"You looked upset when I came in. Is everything alright?"

"Oh, I'm fine," Jenny insisted. "The work's just harder sometimes than I expected and the property is quite isolated, so I'm just feeling a bit overwhelmed. And relieved to be in town, around people, for a few hours."

"I didn't mean to pry," Luke said apologetically, now realizing she and Betsy could have been talking about something that was none of his business.

"It's OK, really. I had to bring my boss in for a doctor's appointment and thought I'd catch up with Betsy while I wait. I haven't seen her for a few weeks."

"Are you sure you don't want me to speak to Peg?" commented Betsy, picking up their previous conversation.

"No, no, Betsy, really, I'm fine. Just a little touch of nerves. So many animals to deal with, I'm just not used to all the different noises and activities. Wolves howling so close to the house just sort of tipped me over the edge."

At that, she glanced at her watch and pulled back from the other two.

"Oh dear, look at that! Peg will be done with her tests in a just few minutes. I need to get up to the hospital to fetch her. See you later Betsy, and nice to meet you Luke," she said with a smile as she turned for the door.

"Poor girl," muttered Betsy as Jenny left the shop.

But before Luke could question her about what Jenny had said about wolves howling, a customer yanked the door open and entered with such determination that Betsy immediately headed his direction.

Luke waved a silent goodbye and headed out.

Chapter 24

Sunday 14 January 11:25 pm

Coroner Debra Wallace had arrived by float plane from Victoria just before noon the day after the attack. She'd had to get up very early to accommodate the rushed trip, made at the behest of Mayor Mutts herself. She'd ensconced herself in the basement morgue of the tiny Tofino Hospital to do the autopsy on the remains of Mitch Rodgers and followup interviews with witnesses.

Since this death was a presumed animal attack, she knew she had to determine what kind of animal had been involved. The initial assumption that it was a bear attack was confirmed through interviews with the two responding constables. However, the state of the body as well as evidence collected at the scene and interviews with all others involved in the recovery process were less conclusive.

The information offered during her long conversation with RCMP wildlife specialist Luke Robinson had been especially concerning, as had her confidential interview with the Parks Canada wildlife conflict specialist.

Under questioning that got increasingly probing, Chelsea Kettle had finally admitted that there had been several serious close calls with wolves on the beaches and park trails over the last few months that had not been reported to the public. In years past, such incidents generally only resulted in generic warnings for increased vigilance and respect from Parks visitors. However, these recent incidents had spooked some visitors so badly that Kettle had taken to handing out free canisters of bear spray to make them feel safer and ensure their cooperation.

Debra had been shocked to learn that such threatening and potentially dangerous encounters with wolves had generated such a nonchalant response from the Parks official.

"What was the purpose of keeping all this quiet?" asked the coroner, trying not to sound confrontational.

"Well, we know the myth of wolves as vicious killers is still rampant—you must know that even today, wolves get mislabelled as cunning and dangerous predators that people have reason to fear. We take the position here at the Park that wolves are simply trying to survive and that such encounters, while frightening in the moment, are probably just individual animals caught off-guard by Park visitors.

"We calmly remind visitors who experience such encounters that wolves have a right to protect their young, or their food, which people might not be aware of because it's out of their view in the background. We council visitors frightened by such incidents that publicly reporting these encounters, even if they do so quite innocently as exciting experiences online, might cause some people to over-react and call for Park wolves to be killed. Invariably, none of our visitors want wolves to be killed just for being here, so they agree to keep quiet."

"But handing out free bear spray is a new response to these encounters, is that correct?" asked Debra, keeping her eyes down to shield the consternation she was afraid they might reveal.

"Yes, in consultation with my supervisors and our First Nations partners, it was decided that some of our guests were sufficiently frightened by their experiences—or by what they'd overheard other visitors describe after encounters—that something more proactive was required to ensure compliance," Kettle replied. "We take our conservation obligations seriously here."

"Thank you for your frankness, Ms. Kettle," Debra said noncommittally. "I think that's all I need from you. I'm sure that dealing with Park visitors under these circumstances can't have been easy for you."

***

Debra had finished her meetings earlier that night and was now in her motel room, evaluating the evidence and information she'd gathered about Mitch's attack. Given the circumstances, she was under real pressure to produce a preliminary cause of death by the next morning.

There were no clear animal tracks among the photos taken at the scene of the attack, but the drag marks and disturbance of the soil suggested to her that more than one animal had been involved. Also, Mitch actually looked like he'd been subject to a tug-of-war, with clothing torn from various parts of his body strewn about the area. There were bite marks on his head, neck, left arm, and both legs. Muscle tissue was missing from his right thigh, left calf, and abdomen.

It would take weeks to write up her final report describing the evidence and her recommendations for preventing future deaths. But she eventually decided that her preliminary determination would have to be that this death was the result of a wolf attack. Or, to be more precise, an attack by wolves, probably more than two. She knew it wouldn't be a popular decision and she'd have to be prepared for blowback from wolf activists within the community, especially Parks personel. And eventually, vitriol from activists around the world.

With that charming prospect in mind, she poured herself two mini-bottles of scotch from the motel fridge and tried to relax before attempting to sleep. Knowing what she'd face tomorrow, she'd fair better if she got some rest but she wasn't especially optimistic that would happen.

Animal attacks usually gave her nightmares.

Chapter 25

Monday 15 January 2:15 pm

A couple of enterprising tourists from Victoria had tried to beat the weekend crowds by arriving Monday morning.

The two determined surfers, brothers Jace and Jamie Pritchard, had spent a cold day sleeping in their van in the beachfront parking lot at Long Beach after driving most of the night. Although sleeping in the van was technically against Park rules, no one had come around to run them off.

The pair woke up in the early afternoon and watched the falling tide as they prepared a simple hot meal on a two-burner camp stove. They'd come equipped with their own gear and had originally planned to start surfing in the early morning darkness and continue until dawn broke on the gently sloping sands of Long Beach.

However, as often was the case with their adventures, weather got in their way.

Heavy snow in the mountains had delayed their arrival and they'd had to adjust. Now they were gearing themselves up for riding the waves into the darkness instead of out of it.

As they ate, the two argued vigorously whether to simply wait another night and surf the next morning as planned but eventually agreed it was just too cold for any more sleeping in the van. It was now or never. They'd come too far to go home without having some kind of adventure.

A combination of headlamps and glowstick wrist bands gave them just enough light to get started. They each had a strap-on waterproof flare, just in case, and their boards were festooned with reflective tape.

Unfortunately, the waves were larger and more violent than they'd anticipated. They struggled while paddling out to where the waves rose to their breaking point, especially Jamie, the younger and less experienced of the two.

The darkness made it harder to spot a good wave but Jace shouted that surfing in the dark was the thrill, hardly anyone ever did it. After a shaky first ride in, they were both thrown into a pounding surf so strong it knocked the wind out of them.

They kept at it but after four runs, they had exhausted themselves fighting the raging sea in the darkness.

After the last nasty spill, Jamie pleaded with his brother for a break, so they paddled toward shore. Jace suddenly stopped and sat up on his board, signalling Jamie to stop. He looked towards shore and pointed, without comment.

Ahead of them on the beach—strung out along the entire length of visible shoreline and back-lit slightly by the paleness of the sand—were the silhouettes of dozens of animals that looked like tall, skinny dogs, except for the one in the middle of the row that was plainly all-white. Suddenly the white one laid down, facing out to sea and the rest followed suit.

After a few minutes, the animals hadn't moved but the wash of the waves had carried the boys' boards closer in. It was suddenly apparent to Jace what they were up against.

"Shit! Those are wolves!" he shouted. "Look at them all! We have to go back out."

"I don't think I can!" pleaded Jamie, breathless with exertion and fear.

"We have to! Just look at them. Just waiting for us to come in. No way. We don't stand a chance against that many."

Jace abruptly turned his board around and started paddling frantically out to sea. With a groan, Jamie tried to follow but didn't have the strength to get very far.

"I can't!" yelled Jamie, struggling to get his board turned around. "Jace! My arms are rubber! Help me!"

Jace shook his head in annoyance but turned his board around and headed in to meet up with his brother.

Jace pulled himself up to a sitting position and looked back towards shore. The squadron of hunters that had been waiting patiently for an opportunity to pounce were still there.

"We'll just have to wait them out!" he shouted to Jamie. "They'll eventually get tired and leave."

"How long is that going to take?" answered Jamie. "I'm really scared."

"Yeah, I know, but we don't have a choice, do we?" Jace called out.

Jace paddled over to Jamie's board and gave his brother a quick hug.

However, try as they might, they simply didn't have the strength to keep the waves from washing them closer and closer to the beach. Eventually, the fins of the boards scrapped bottom and they realized they were almost to shore.

There was no movement or sounds ahead of them. They'd missed the fact that the wolves had split up into two groups that now waited in the darkness either side of their landing point.

"I can't see them anymore," said Jamie. "They must be gone. Let's get out of here!"

The pair got off their boards and picked them up. But as they struggled to wade through the shallows near the water's edge, they realized the wolves were now advancing diagonally towards them.

In shock, Jace dropped his board. Jamie quickly followed suit. They turned back to the sea but the ankle-deep water impeded their escape. They heard splashing behind them as the wolves leapt through the surf.

Jamie fell face-first into the water as the big white wolf hit him from behind and seconds later, Jace fell as well. The surfboard tether-straps snapped.

The pair were dead by drowning by the time several of the wolves dragged them to shore. Taking turns at the work, the pack managed to pull the brothers up the sand dunes and into the scrubby woods beyond.

Within an hour, the churned-up sand, drag marks, and wolf tracks that would have told the story of the surfside attack were temporarily erased by falling snow—and when the snow finally melted, no one thought anything of the strange marks in the sand.

The boys' surf boards bobbed in the waves all night until they were eventually swept out to sea. The illegally-parked van was towed to an impound lot.

It was almost a week before someone connected a missing person's report on the Pritchard brothers to the owner of the van and the battered surfboards that had washed up several beaches further north.

Chapter 26

Monday 15 January 7:00 pm

After news of the Tonquin Trail attack on Mitch Rodgers had spread through town, Mayor Mutts called a town meeting to announce the preliminary results of the autopsy, to be held at the Community Centre. It was really the only building in town with enough room for several hundred people *and* their vehicles.

Baylou had arrived very early on her bike and waited outside, around the corner from the main entrance and beyond the cone of mega-watt luminosity shining from the lights over the doors, sensing she would not be welcome inside. She was restless but alert, constantly scanning the darkness beyond.

She gave a small wave to Willie as he arrived with his father and an older man that she recognized as Uncle Jack, whom she had met a few times over the years. But she shrank even further into the darkness when she saw Luke arrive a few minutes later, unsure that she should let him know she was there.

Soon, there was a flurry of cars and trucks pulling into the multi-tiered gravel parking lot. Even the lot cut into the hill above and behind the hall, seldom used outside of really large events, filled right up. People streamed into the building, chattering excitedly. Soon, the trucks stopped arriving and someone pulled the big doors closed, signalling the start of the meeting.

It was very cold and smelled like it might snow. She knew she had a long, lonely wait in the dark ahead of her but she didn't mind. She's spent a lot of time in the dark alone over her life and she knew that this time, someone had to keep watch.

***

Inside, Luke saw Willie at the front of the hall standing next to a strapping young man with black hair down to his shoulders. He sauntered over to the pair, as Willie was the only person he saw that he knew. Willie waved Luke over as soon as he noticed him approaching.

"Luke, this is cousin Micah. He won Ukee Days first prize Paddling for Tuna! Three years in a row!" said Willie loudly, almost breathless with pride.

Luke stepped forward to shake Micah's hand.

"Hi Micah, I'm Luke Robinson. Nice to meet you. I've heard of the some of the crazy things that go on at the Ukee Days Festival in Ucluelet. That's in the summer, right? But what on earth is 'Paddling for Tuna'? A contest?"

Micah laughed out loud and looked affectionately down at Willie.

"Our way of paying tribute to our ancestors. They used to hunt for giant Bluefin tuna on the west coast, including Ucluelet. In the old days, big tuna, 2 or 3 metres long, would come close to shore at the end of summer. Fastest fish in the sea, they say. Strongest men in the village would chase after them, using canoes used for hunting whales. They'd harpoon a giant fish and it would tow the canoe way up to the top of the inlet. When it got tired and gave up, the men would have to paddle all the way back to the village."

"Wow, I never heard of that," said Luke, genuinely impressed. "So, how do you duplicate the old hunt for Ukee Days? Is there a giant mechanical fish to chase, like the shark they used in the movie Jaws? I know about giant Bluefin from my days in Newfoundland, they're enormous!"

Micah laughed again, one of the warmest, friendliest sounds Luke had ever heard outside the Arctic.

"No, nothing like that," the articulate young man continued. "It's just a race, really, but we use an 8 metre freight canoe and two paddlers. We start out at the seaplane boat launch and paddle up the inlet, around the island and back. Hard work for two men in a canoe that big. Fastest time wins one of those big, commercial-sized cans of tuna."

Now it was Luke's turn to laugh. "Couldn't you just have a contest to go out and catch one?"

"No, no, wouldn't work. Big tuna don't come here anymore. They say there hasn't been any around for more than a hundred years. We only know about them because archaeologists found their bones in old village middens up and down the island—and a few elders who

164

heard stories about the old hunts finally passed them along."

The sound in the hall changed perceptively at that point, which Luke took to mean the meeting would soon begin.

"Who are you here with, Willie?" Luke whispered in the boy's ear. "Did your dad bring you?"

"Yeah, he's over there, with Uncle Jack," said Willie. "Not my real uncle, you know that, right? Hard to explain. An elder, from Opitsat. The reserve. He's going to speak later, for the village. People are really upset, lots of talk. I don't know, I think I heard some mothers saying it's not safe anymore to let kids play outside."

Just then, there was a call to order. Willie and Micah hurried off to join their relatives. Luke saw Blake near the front with an empty seat beside her and pushed through the crowd to join her. She patted the empty seat when she saw him approach. She was sitting near the end of the row next to the two other officers that had helped recover Mitch Rodgers' body.

Detachment-head Bob Hammond and several other people Luke didn't recognize were already onstage, as the mayor held the microphone and waited for the crowd to settle down.

After a short introduction by the mayor and a summary of the police investigation by Sergeant Hammond into what had happened to Mitch, the coroner got up to give her preliminary cause of death. There was a gasp from the crowd when they heard wolves were probably to blame. Luke noticed Hammond shaking his head at this reaction.

Gus Allerod, a local artist known to be a lover of wolves and a vocal activist for wolf conservation, bolted to his feet.

"That all sounds more like a bear to me. Why do people always want to blame wolves? Even if it was more than one animal, it could have been a sow with cubs!" he shouted, from the middle of the crowd.

"You're right, in theory," replied the coroner, trying to stay calm but having to raise her voice above the rumbling from the crowd.

"But you should know as well as everyone here that the cold this winter has driven all the bears into hibernation. And if it hadn't been such a good year for berries last summer, I might agree with you that it *could* have been bears coming out now because they didn't get fat enough last fall," she added firmly.

"What about wolf-dog hybrids?" shouted another resident. "We keep hearing about hybrids, how dangerous and unpredictable they can be. Maybe some idiot let a bunch of them loose in the woods to fend for themselves when they got to be too much to handle."

"Entirely possible," admitted the coroner. "It will be days before I get the DNA results back from the lab, and they might tell us if it was wild wolves or hybrids involved. However, those tests aren't always definitive, so let's not leap to conclusions one way or the other."

The wildlife specialist from the National Park, who was seated on-stage beside the mayor, asked for the microphone. Introduced as Chelsea Kettle, she stood and faced the crowd.

"I agree that this behaviour sounds abnormal for wild wolves. We've never had a fatal attack by wolves reported in the Park," she stated emphatically. "Wolf-dog hybrids have been reported in a number of locations around the island over the last several decades, so it's not inconceivable that this situation is what we're dealing with here.

"That makes it even more critical for people to be careful with their garbage and not leave any human food around that they can get into," she added. "Folks may have gotten complacent about dealing with garbage over the last few months because the bears aren't around, but sloppy garbage hygiene could be attracting hybrids to town."

There was groan and a wave of even louder muttering from the crowd. Garbage was a contentious community issue and some residents were tired of the relentless nagging from all sides. Most often, they insisted, it was tourists and new-comers who caused most of the problems, so the constant hectoring of long-time residents solved nothing.

Then the hall went quiet as Uncle Jack stood up in his seat at the front of the hall and moved onstage. He took the microphone, said something in his native language that sounded something like a prayer and then switched to English. His message was brief.

"Good evening. I say to my people and to you, my neighbours, that wolves have been a sacred part of our lives for thousands of years. We know each other, we respect each other. They are our brothers. We both earn a living from the forest and the sea. Our solemn vow to co-exist benefits everyone. The wolf knows this, we know this.

"A long, long time ago, many wolves that fell on hard times came to our village and broke our pledge. Our children were snatched from the beach and taken into the forest. It was a great tragedy for our people.

"We learned then how to re-connect with our wolf brothers, to rekindle the trust and respect we need to co-exist. I urge you all tonight to do the same. This is a time for hope and forgiveness, for reverence and compassion. Thank you."

Luke turned to Betsy and whispered in her ear, "What do you think he means by that?"

"I have no idea," she murmured back, noting that some First Nations elders in the hall were earnestly nodding their heads in agreement. "But it's interesting that something like these recent attacks seem to have happened before. Yet he doesn't really say how it was resolved."

With that, the meeting seemed to be over, although there was no formal announcement that it had concluded.

Someone opened the doors to release the community members into the night to reveal that it had started to snow while they were busy inside.

Angry shouting from the parking lot caused a silence to settle over the chatty crowd as people shuffled towards the doors.

Luke recognized the voice as Baylou's. Realizing Blake was still beside him, he pushed aggressively through the throng and out the door to see what was happening. With Blake trailing behind, he finally got to the bottom of the stairs and looked off towards the edge of the forest where the yelling seemed to be coming from.

He could barely see Baylou off at the edge of the parking lot but could hear her repeat herself over and over, as if she were warning off someone, or something, hiding unseen in the trees beyond. She just stood there, frantically waving her arms.

"Oh no you don't! Don't you dare! Not your place! Devils! Go! Go!"

It reminded Luke of the incident on the beach a few days ago, when she'd told him she'd seen the eyes of wolves.

Could there really be wolves out there in the forest, so close to all these people?

As she finished her tirade, Baylou hopped on her bike and headed out of the parking lot and down the hill through the snow without so much as a backward glance.

Chapter 27

Monday 15 January 9:20 pm

"What the hell was that all about?" Blake whispered in Luke's ear, as the crowd stood in stunned silence watching Baylou's retreat.

"I don't think there's anything to worry about but I'll tell you later," Luke whispered back, as the people around them finally burst into excited chatter. "We'd better let these folks get out of here."

Blake needed to talk to her colleagues from the detachment and Luke wanted to see if Willie might introduce him to Uncle Jack, so they both headed back inside.

As Luke stood just inside the doors scanning the crowd for Willie's small frame and white baseball cap, he became aware of a familiar-looking dark-haired woman standing beside him who seemed to be doing the same thing. Seeing an opportunity to turn an acquaintance into a friend, he took a step towards her.

"Almost impossible to find someone in this mess, isn't it?" he said to Jenny in a conspiratorial tone from just behind her.

"It's ridiculous!" she exploded in exasperation but when she turned around, her face softened and a smile spread across her face. "Oh, it's you! Luke, isn't it?"

"Yes, that's right. Good to see you again, Jenny."

"I wasn't expecting to see you here. In fact, I didn't expect there would be so many people here period. When I realized how crazy it was getting, I made a special mental note of what Betsy was wearing so I could find her again. But that turned out to be useless strategy!"

"I see your point," replied Luke. "Even a tall person would be hard to pick out in this crowd, let alone someone as small as Betsy."

"Impossible," Jenny clarified. "She went off with some of her friends and she's my ride home. Now I need to get going. I don't have my own car so Betsy offered to bring me tonight. We really wanted to find out what's been going on. A fatal animal attack? Wild, isn't it?"

"Yes, indeed—more than a little concerning," offered Luke.

"That's for sure. But I really need to get back to Peg's. Sorry, I'd better go and check the kitchen, Betsy said something about picking up a baking pan she'd left at bingo. Nice seeing you again."

Jenny flashed him an especially warm smile, then turned and headed into the throng.

"You too," he said, smiling back. But she was already gone.

He watched her until she disappeared behind an especially large man in a plaid jacket.

"Whatcha doing?" asked Willie in a slightly sing-song manner from somewhere around Luke's elbow. The accusatory tone of Willie's question, as well as the smirk on his face, made Luke wonder how long he'd been there.

"Oh, just talking to a neighbour," Luke replied, still a bit distracted by the encounter.

"Pretty," commented Willie, glancing up at Luke with a sly smile.

"Yes, she is," said Luke, grinning back. "She is indeed."

Then Luke seemed to realize why he was there.

"Willie, I wondered if you would mind introducing me to Uncle Jack. Do you think that would be OK?" he asked. "I'd really like to talk to him about the wolves."

"He left. Came with Freddie, on his boat. They had to get back. I came to say bye, my dad wants to leave now."

"OK then, another time perhaps. Thanks for introducing me to your cousin. Maybe I'll see you on the beach later," Luke replied.

As Willie headed towards the doors, Luke looked back into the room and saw it had thinned out considerably. He caught sight of Jenny standing on her own near the stage with her phone to her ear, looking annoyed.

He headed over to see what was the trouble.

"No luck?" he asked.

"I texted her but she's apparently in the middle of a kitchen kafuffle and isn't ready to leave yet. Now Peg's just called. She's getting anxious being home by herself."

"I'd be happy to give you a ride. I live off Mackenzie Beach road, it won't be out of my way," Luke offered.

"Are you sure?" she replied with obvious relief. "That would be a huge help, thank you. Let me just text Betsy and tell her I've found a ride with you so she doesn't have to rush through whatever she's doing."

When she'd finished, Luke led the way into the parking lot, where a couple inches of bright white snow lay over the ground.

"I know it's not very much but I hear even this much snow is unusual for Tofino," he commented as he held the passenger door of his truck open for Jenny.

"Yeah, that's what I keep hearing too," she said with a shiver. "Seems like we've bumped into a whole bunch of unusual."

"You mean the attack?" Luke replied, feigning ignorance. "The coroner's report was disconcerting, for sure."

"I never even imagined wolves would attack people. And "missing muscle tissue" — that means Mitch was eaten, doesn't it?"

Luke glanced over at her, alerted by the tremor in her voice that hadn't been there earlier. He thought she looked a little paler as well but it may have been the outdoor lighting.

"Yes, it does, unfortunately," he replied. "And on top of all the dogs that've been killed or gone missing, I'd have thought the coroner would have shown more concern than she did. *And* the mayor, for that matter."

"Dogs going missing? Do you mean attacked like Mitch? No one said anything about that," Jenny blurted out, her voice rising slightly with fear.

"Well, it's what I've heard but how much is simply rumour, I can't really say. But I passed along to the coroner what I've been told. Some of it came from Betsy. Hasn't she said anything to you?"

"Only bits and pieces," said Jenny, feigning ignorance herself.

"Really?" Luke replied, a bit perplexed. "You must have heard that yelling outside just after the meeting ended? That was a woman named Baylou, who's one of Betsy's artists. Her dog was killed a few weeks ago and she insists it was a wolf. Apparently, some First Nations dogs have disappeared, which they assume have been taken by wolves. And there have been some close calls involving kids with a wolf pack over on the reserve, at Opitsat."

"That's crazy!" Jenny cried. "I had no idea all that was going on. Why didn't the mayor say so?"

"I honestly don't know," Luke said, shaking his head. "Maybe to avoid panic, before we really know what's going on."

Before he could ask her about hearing wolves howling, Luke came to the drive leading to the Menagerie property and turned in. Jenny warned him to watch for potholes but didn't say anything more. He pulled up near the house and stopped.

"Thanks so much for the lift," she said, turning towards him and flashing that warm smile again, leaning over to lay her hand on his arm. "I'm so grateful."

"My pleasure," he replied, smiling back. "Would you like to have lunch sometime, on your day off? I still don't know many people in town and I'm determined to change that," he added tentatively.

"I'd like that," she said fondly. "Can I call you? I'm not sure when I'll be free. It depends a lot on how Peggy is feeling. I don't think I mentioned that she's pregnant and her husband is out of town right now, so she doesn't like being alone."

"I totally understand," he said, reaching into his pocket. Handing her one of his business cards, he said to call when she was free and they'd make a plan to get together.

He watched her walk up to the house and let herself in. She seemed to have a natural gracefulness that most tall women he'd met couldn't quite manage. As if she was strong overall, not just in her hands. Confident. And comfortable around animals, although apparently not wild ones.

He could tell by the racing of his heart that his Christmas triste with Blake had awoken something inside that had been buried for too long. Although he knew better than to get his hopes up, there was just something about this woman. He had a feeling that thoughts of her would keep him awake at night.

As would thoughts about Blake: whether she secretly hoped for more, despite her insistence that their holiday dalliance shouldn't be taken too seriously—and whether he might secretly feel the same.

Chapter 28

Monday 15 January 10:00 pm

Luke found a local weather report online before he went to bed. Apparently, the snow that had started falling during the Tofino town meeting had developed into a full-on blizzard up in the mountains to the east.

There had been two major accidents at the Summit that closed the highway leading into and out of the west coast; the Hump outside Port Alberni had been closed pre-emptively to avoid a similar disaster. Hundreds of cars full of tourists headed for a holiday at the beach, enticed by the forecast of strong winds and big waves, were stranded along the way. Some found motel accommodation while others were taken in by small communities offering places of refuge.

Luke was concerned to hear that the storm was expected to rage into Tuesday morning, which meant both Tofino and Ucluelet were effectively cut off from the outside world. Hurricane-force winds had already grounded flights in and out of the local airport and 15-20ft waves kept boats tethered at their home ports.

Under the circumstances, the coroner wasn't going to be able to get out of Tofino in the morning as expected and would have to stay in town. With the way things were going, Luke hoped that didn't mean there would be more business for her to deal with.

Chapter 29

Tuesday 16 January 8:15 am

Baylou found Willie at the beach. As they often did when it was really stormy, they met in the lee of the tombolo at the north end of Chesterman Beach. Willie had claimed a large flat rock to use as a perch and sat watching the wind whip through the trees onshore.

Baylou leaned her bike against a big tree that had fallen from the slope and sat next to him on his rock.

"People were upset to hear you last night," offered Willie, after several long minutes of silence. "Said you must be drunk."

"Let them talk. I don't care. No one thinking clearly. I know what I saw. Big trouble coming."

"Heard Uncle Jack talking to Papa last night, after we got home," Willie said, his voice barely rising above the roar of the wind. "Thought he went out on the boat but I guess he didn't. He was at our place when we got there, with some others. Usually, they let me listen but I got sent to bed. Pissed me off. Had to crawl down the hall on my belly to listen at the door.

"Uncle Jack said wolves have powerful spirits, so they have to be careful. Something about now we have wolves from outside that don't understand our agreement, how to live together, that they must be greeted with strength. Said these wolves have come looking for food, think we're prey. And he got all serious, told the same story he said at the meeting, that this happened before, a long time ago. Before we had guns. Said wolves we lived with forever suddenly had hard times, broke our agreement. Took our kids."

"Never heard that before, about taking kids, before last night," Baylou said with concern.

"He said we learned from that, to be wary—show the wolf respect but don't trust him completely. Show him we value our kids, never let him think we're weak and helpless as young deer. Not sure I get what it means, really, but then he said something about this being the way for us to live together."

"Makes sense, if you think about it—have respect but don't turn your back," said Baylou, nodding. "What else?"

"Something about the wolves now, the ones here right now, not being the wolves of our ancestors. They came from far away, because of hard times. Desperately hungry now, he said. He told Papa we must respect and understand this—desperate wolves, like desperate people, do things they wouldn't normally do. I guess that makes sense too, right?"

"Yeah, I think so," agreed Baylou.

"Then he went back to saying something about showing wolves it's not OK to gang up together to take our kids.

That when they run out of dogs to eat, they *will* take our kids. Kind of scary."

"Yeah, really scary," Baylou added, nodding again.

"When Papa asked what to do, Uncle Jack said we've been too weak—now we must send these wolves away by force. Only message they understand is the loss of their own, he said. Any that remain will tell others we aren't weak, we won't stand for our kids being taken. Maybe one day, later, we can live together again."

"Did he say how long?" asked Baylou, frowning.

"Papa asked that too but Uncle Jack just said 'later'," Willie replied with frustration. "Then Papa said some band members don't get that these are not usual times, that Uncle Jack is the one who knows the right thing to do. And something about white men thinking they understand everything when they don't. And then Uncle Jack said something I didn't really get. That by fighting for our kid's lives, we embrace our original selves. What do you think he meant by that?"

After staring off at the wind-wept trees onshore for a few moments, Baylou looked back at Willie.

"People sometimes have to fight for what they really value, even if most of the time they're not fighters. And maybe, that not all stories the elders know are told to others—sometimes, important knowledge waits for the right moment to be shared with just the right people."

"What are they going to do, though? I still don't get it!"

"I think they're going to try and kill the wolves," whispered Baylou. "Most of them, anyway. Don't know how. But Uncle Jack seems to have a plan."

"But why didn't he say that last night, at the meeting?"

"I think some spirits—like wolves—are so powerful that only the strongest people can handle them. Sometimes, only one elder—like Uncle Jack—will decide who needs to know what to do and who will do it. Keeps everyone safe. Not everybody needs to know. Just better that way."

"What do I do now?" asked Willie anxiously. "Can't let on that I know, can I?"

"Just do what your dad says, he'll keep you safe," she said patiently. "If you see strange things happening, people coming and going, just pretend you don't notice. All it means is the people who need to take care of this are doing what they need to do. It's grownup business you don't need to worry about."

"I'm not a baby," Willie objected loudly. "Don't need to be protected!"

"No, you're not a little kid. But sometimes, it's just better that only a few people to know what's going on. Your dad will tell you all about it, when the time is right."

"Do you know when it's going to happen, whatever's going on?" he asked.

"No, but I have an idea. What I'd do if it were up to me. Trust Uncle Jack, he'll do what's right."

.

Chapter 30

Tuesday 16 January 8:45 am

Luke tapped lightly on the door of Blake's trailer, empty coffee cup in hand.

"It's open!" she shouted from within.

Luke entered, cup first. It had become a ritual for them on days she worked an afternoon shift to have coffee together before she headed off to the gym.

"Do you have time to talk about the meeting last night?" he said, as she silently poured his coffee.

"Yes, but not long. I promised to meet up with Cole this morning for a workout and I'm not sure yet what condition the roads are going to be in."

"Yeah, the snow's deeper than I thought it would be. Must be five or six inches out there," Luke replied.

Then he launched into a bit of a tirade.

"What is it with your boss? Why is he so fixated on the idea that the attack on Mitch was done by a bear? Really, there's no evidence to support that conclusion."

"I don't know, Luke. Really. I wouldn't have pegged him as one of those animal-lovers who believe wolves can do no wrong, but it's looking more and more like he might be. There's been a number of wildlife incidents we've handled since I got here but most of them actually did involve bears. However, when I think back on it, he's always underplayed the few wolf incidents we've had."

"I don't like it," said Luke tersely. "It makes me wonder if we can trust him to act appropriately if the shit hits the fan."

"Yeah, you and me both," countered Blake. "But we don't know yet if we really have anything to worry about."

"Yeah, I guess you're right," said Luke, finishing his coffee and setting it on the counter next to the sink.

Just then his phone rang, so he gave Blake a quick wave goodbye as he walked off, answering Jenny's call as he opened the door to his own trailer.

***

Three hours later, he set off to pick up Jenny for lunch. He'd been surprised to hear from her so soon, but she explained that Peg had only just told her she had a friend coming out to the farm for the afternoon, leaving Jenny unexpectedly available.

Jenny had apologized for the short notice but he said he was happy to follow through on his offer and would pick her up at 12:30. However, that left him scrambling to think of exactly where to take her, something he hadn't considered when he'd made the invitation last night.

His truck handled the snowy roads without trouble. She was waiting for him in the same spot he'd dropped her off last night, dressed for the weather.

"I thought we could go to the restaurant at Tin Wis," he said, as she climbed into his truck. "It's got a good view and I hear the food is excellent. Plus, it may be one of the only places still open after the storm. It's not far."

"That sounds great. I haven't been there yet," she said with quiet excitement.

"How's Peg? Was she OK when you got home last night?" he asked.

"Oh, yes—just a little anxious because she got overtired yesterday. She's expecting twins, did I tell you that? So, she gets tired easily even though she's got another couple months until the birth. That's if she manages to go full term with them, which may not happen. They could come early."

"She must really appreciate your help."

"Yeah, she does. It's not the most glamourous job in the world but at least I feel useful."

Jenny went silent after that as Luke turned down the dedicated road to the resort and parked the truck. As they entered through the main doors into the lobby, they could see through into the dining room ahead.

They were given seats in the middle of the huge wall of windows looking onto Mackenzie Beach. Although another half dozen or so tables were also occupied, they were so scattered around the room that they all had more than a modicum of privacy.

The pair chatted amicably while they chose their meal and waited for it to arrive but Luke sensed that Jenny was struggling to sound carefree. She deflected most of his questions and turned them back on him, leaving him telling her more about himself than he'd intended.

At one point, he happened to glance over at the main doors, conscious of the automatic doors opening and then feeling like he was being watched. There he thought he saw a big white wolf standing stalk-still outside the entryway, looking directly at him. He stared back for a second, then shook his head and turned away in disbelief. When he looked back, it was gone.

He must have imagined it, with all the wolf-talk. He gave his attention back to Jenny.

She seemed relieved when her food arrived and quickly gave it her full attention. After a few moments, he glanced over at her, his mouth open to ask if her fish was as good as it looked but changed his mind as soon as he saw the tension in her face.

"Is something wrong?" he asked gently, reaching over to touch her hand lightly. "You look miserable."

She put her fork down and looked up at him, tears suddenly welling up in her eyes.

"I'm sorry! It's not you—really, it's not. But I think I have to tell you something," she blurted out.

"I vowed to Peg I wouldn't tell anyone but now that I know how involved you are in this wolf business, I don't think I can keep that promise."

"Did something happen at the farm?" asked Luke earnestly. "If so, I think you should tell me. It could be important."

Tears now running down her face, Jenny spilled the story of the wolf attacks, starting with the incidents involving the chickens, emus and the pig, and ending with an especially graphic rendition of the slaughter of the goats four nights before, the one which Baylou had witnessed.

Luke reached over and wiped the tears from her face with his thumb, then gently cupped her chin in his hand.

"It will be OK. Peg will forgive you for telling, it would get out anyway eventually," he said, using the most soothing tone he possessed.

"Peg stopped all the weekend openings, says locals would notice in an instant that all the goats were gone," Jenny whispered.

Then Luke sat back and let his professional voice kick in.

"So, Baylou's actually *seen* the wolves in action," he said with awe, as if a puzzle piece had suddenly fallen into place. "That explains why she's been so adamant the last few days that the wolf problem is out of control."

"It was truly horrifying to watch—the goats screaming, blood everywhere. Peg saw it all but I only caught it half way through, which was bad enough," Jenny admitted.

Just then Luke's phone rang. He saw it was Hammond calling and told Jenny he should take it.

The call lasted only a few moments. Luke mostly listened and gave a few short answers, then hung up.

As Jenny looked at him quizzically, he explained as he rose from his chair.

"We'll have to go. Apparently, a couple of young girls have gone missing from one of the resorts at Mackenzie Beach and Bob Hammond is organizing a search party. I could just walk from here because it's just down the beach but I'll take you home first. I don't know how long I'll be."

"What does 'missing' mean?" asked Jenny, now also on her feet and struggling into her coat.

"I don't know. It could be runaways or something more sinister. I don't think they know yet. But you should be with Peg."

He took a few steps to close the gap between them. Jenny looked up at him, tears welling in her eyes again. He wrapped his arms around her and gave her a reassuring hug.

"You'll be fine. Don't worry," he whispered into her hair. "I'll call you later and let you know what's happened."

Jenny leaned into him and they stood like that for a few minutes. Pulling away slightly, he brushed his lips against her cheek then gently took her hand and led her purposefully out to the parking lot.

It was a short ride back to the Menagerie. There was no time for a long goodbye—she jumped out of the truck as soon as he came to a skewed stop behind a car Jenny didn't recognize that was parked by the back door of Peg's house. He raised his hand in a brief wave as he made a tight turn and took off back down the driveway.

Jenny knew she'd have to tell Peg their secret was out but it could wait a few hours until her visitor had left. She took off her coat and headed to the kitchen to bake something, suddenly smiling as she remembered the feeling of his lips on her face and her hand in his.

Chapter 31

Tuesday 16 January 2:00 pm

Luke retraced most of his earlier drive except this time he took Mackenzie Beach Road all the way down to its oceanside terminus. He was waved through a police roadblock and pulled into the parking lot of the resort and campsite complex that dominated this section of the beach.

He spotted Sergeant Hammond in a huddle with some civilians at the side of what looked to be the resort's office building. He approached the group but stood out of earshot until Hammond had finished and waved the others away.

Luke moved closer as Hammond looked over at him, raising both hands in exasperation.

"What happened?" asked Luke.

"I'm not really sure. Apparently, last night around 7:00, two young girls that were part of a group here on a short vacation came up here to office to get more firewood for their cabin but didn't return. Their friends had assumed the girls had decided to drive into town and just didn't bother to let them know, so didn't call the detachment to report them missing until after midnight. The auxiliary officer who took the call promised to check accident reports and get back to them if there was any news.

"However, the officer's notes only reflected a call to check for reports of accidents involving the girls' car, not the fact that two people were overdue and presumed missing. And because there had been some kind of on-going argument during their stay, by morning the friends had convinced themselves the girls had simply gone home early and left them to pack up their stuff.

"It wasn't until late this morning, when the friends came up to the parking lot to do their check-out, that they realized the girls' car was still there. Then they saw the sign they'd all missed the previous day, announcing that the office was closing early that night because of the town meeting. That means no one was actually here last night when the girls came up for firewood—there was no one around at all."

"Any idea what happened to them?" asked Luke warily.

"Well, obviously, they either went somewhere on foot or possibly, left in a vehicle someone else was driving. At first, we organized a search around all of the cabins at the resort and along the beach out front, but found nothing. Fresh snow has covered any tracks that might have told us which way they might have gone. I thought if they were looking for wood they might have walked down the road into the campground area, so I've got Blake leading a team searching there right now. But it's a huge area and it's going to take a while."

"Maybe I can help," offered Luke graciously. "All my years in the Arctic have given me some experience dealing with snow-covered evidence. I've found that sometimes, if you do it carefully, you can brush away the top layer of snow to reveal tracks below. The problem you've got here is that a lot of people and vehicles have been moving through the parking lot. But if we look at the undisturbed areas around their car, we might get lucky."

After Hammond pointed out which car belonged to the missing girls, Luke went over to a nearby cedar tree and cut off a broom-length branch. Then he approached the driver's side of the car using a trail that others had made in the snow and started brushing the top layer of undisturbed snow away with the feathery tips of the cedar fronds.

He worked his way around to the back of the car and patiently moved toward the centre of the parking lot. After more than half an hour of light brushing, he suddenly looked up and scanned the lot for Hammond, who was on the phone but still watching him.

"Here!" he exclaimed, clearing the snow away a bit more vigorously in an expanding arc.

What he'd revealed were some obscured blood and animal track evidence of the attack that had taken place. As Luke worked the snow layer, he found some drag marks, more wolf tracks and a few bits of torn clothing leading off into the bush beside the parking lot.

"Definitely wolves," he told Hammond in a quiet voice. "Judging from the number of individual paw prints, I'd say more than one, perhaps many more. The bodies were dragged into that wooded area and probably consumed there. I'd say it's very unlikely the girls were still alive when they were taken from the parking lot."

Hammond just looked at Luke in stunned silence.

"I think it's highly likely you've got a double wolf attack fatality on your hands, Bob. That would make it three deaths altogether. This is really serious."

Just then, Luke looked up to see Blake's truck coming towards them from the campsite road on the other side of the cul-de-sac. She pulled up next to them and rolled down her window and looked directly at Hammond.

"We've found something, sir. Not to do with the missing girls, it's something else. Looks like two people staked out a campsite at the farthest end of the property. Owner says it's news to him—campground is closed during the winter. Staff check the bathrooms several times a week but as far as he knows, haven't found any evidence of illegal campers.

"The state of the gear we found suggests it's been there more than a week—backpacks soaking wet from the rain we had last week, soggy sleeping bags, tents fallen over. Ravens have done a number on the backpacks, scattered a lot of the food around. No vehicle. I've got Cole going through it all to see if he can find any identification."

Hammond just shook his head and looked at Luke.

"I know the world is full of idiots, but why do they all have to come here on vacation?" he ranted in quiet exasperation. "Let's just hope these ones thought they'd have a free lark but something scared them so badly they took off without bothering to pack up. Not the first time, probably won't be the last."

When Hammond turned his attention back to Blake, Luke looked directly at her and raised a questioning eyebrow.

"We don't have time for that now, Blake," Hammond huffed. "It looks like the missing girls were attacked by wolves right here in the parking lot. Pull your team out of the campsite and get them searching that patch of forest over there for any remains."

They all looked over at the wooded area in reverent silence for a minute or so, until the mood was broken by Hammond.

"Damn! It looks like we'll have more work for the coroner before she has a chance to leave town," he sighed.

Chapter 32

Wednesday 17 January 7:00 pm

Coroner Debra Wallace squirmed in her chair on the small stage of the community centre as the mayor and Sergeant Hammond tried to bring some order to the assembled crowd. She hadn't looked forward to this meeting and had warned the mayor it might get ugly. And she'd been right.

The place was packed and from the get-go, the audience was restless and vocal. The hastily-arranged town meeting had been called after she'd spent the day examining evidence and come to the preliminary conclusion that the two girls missing from the Mackenzie Beach Resort had been killed and eaten by wolves.

Wallace had been taken to the site early that morning, where she'd collected some isolated body parts and bits of clothing from an area deep in the forest beyond the resort parking lot. After an examination of the confusing mass of animal tracks, she'd managed to isolate several clear wolf tracks belonging to different individuals. She couldn't say for sure how many wolves had actually participated in the attack but concluded there had been at least three, perhaps many more.

After conveying this information at the meeting, the crowd had exploded. Nothing specific could be heard above the general din of people talking and shouting out questions but the atmosphere was anger heavily tinged with fear.

Suddenly, the double doors flew open and two couples left the building with their children in tow. After a few moments, another dozen followed them out into the night.

Someone pulled the doors closed behind them as Sergeant Hammond demanded everyone take their seats. As the crowd quieted down, the Mayor stood up to try and get the meeting back on track.

It was only then they heard the screams from the upper parking lot just beyond the emergency side doors of the hall. Just one scream at first, then three or four. A car door slammed, then another. More screaming as a truck engine fired up and a woman burst through the front doors of the hall.

"Help!" she shouted hysterically, her terror apparent. "Wolves in the back lot! Pulling kids into the woods. They need help!"

Hammond and his officers, including Blake, bolted out the emergency exit doors that opened onto the upper parking lot. There could still hear screaming coming from that direction.

Luke had been at the back of the hall due to his late arrival and by the time he made his way to the emergency exit, someone had closed the other doors behind the hysterical woman. A crowd surrounded her on that side of the hall, partly to console her but also to find out what was going on.

Luke slipped out the emergency exit onto the landing and pulled it almost-closed behind him. Beyond, illuminated just enough by the headlights of a vehicle at the far end, he saw that several men carrying children were running through the parked cars on their way back to the hall.

He reached back and pushed the door open again for the people that Hammond and Cole were herding up the stairs. He guided them in and shouted encouragement to another group Blake was shepherding towards him.

As Blake led her group into the safety of the hall, Luke looked up and saw a large man limping hurriedly around the cars towards the hall, cradling a screaming child in his arms. As they reached the base of the stairs, Luke saw both were covered in blood. Hammond and Cole helped the man up the stairs.

As soon as they reached the landing, someone announcing he was a doctor, who appeared to have been standing right behind Luke, pushed past him to take charge of the emergency. Hammond and Cole stood aside as the doctor move in beside the injured pair.

"It's alright, you're safe now," said the doctor sympathetically, laying his hand on the bleeding man's arm.

"I'm Doctor Aaron McTavish, I work at the hospital," he said calmly, following up with a practiced string of questions and reassuring statements. "Is this your daughter? Let me have a look at her leg, will you? I think we need to stop that bleeding. Is it alright if I take her from you? I'll just take her into the kitchen where the light is better. It's going to be OK, I'll take good care of her, I promise."

The man gulped air and nodded his assent as he looked down at his daughter's leg in horror. Below the knee, it was a bleeding mass of mangled flesh and exposed bone. What he couldn't see—but that Luke and the doctor did—was that part of her scalp was also hanging loose and bleeding profusely.

Uttering more soothing and encouraging words, the doctor gently extracted the screaming child from the man's arms and disappeared with the terrified girl towards the kitchen. Most of the people standing nearby turned and followed the pair into the bowels of the hall.

As the crowd around him cleared, Luke turned his attention back to the big man, whose left leg and arm were also bleeding. Someone surreptitiously placed a first aid kit in Luke's hand, then disappeared.

"Here, let's get you out of the cold and take a look at your leg," Luke said gently, holding up the kit for emphasis. He got under the man's uninjured arm and helped him hobble inside and swung a nearby chair around to get him seated. Bob Hammond followed them into the hall and nodded to Luke his permission to take the lead as Cole pushed back the other chairs to give them room.

"You need to try and catch your breath," coached Luke calmly. "Slow down, take some deep breaths. That's right, that's better. You're bleeding a bit but we'll get you fixed up. The doctor is taking care of your daughter. It's going to be OK."

Blake silently motioned for Cole to give her his coat and then stepped forward without comment to place it over the injured man's broad shoulders.

"Let's see what's going on here," Luke said tenderly, cutting the lower portion of the man's jeans away, revealing several deep bite marks on the thickest part of the calf. "I think you're going to need some stitches but let's get a bandage on it for now."

Luke started wrapping the man's leg with gauze but stopped briefly to look up at him, making eye contact.

"What's your name?" he asked compassionately.

"Judd. Judd Burke," the big man replied, forcing his voice under control.

"You're a brave man, Judd," Luke said firmly. "If you're feeling up to it, do you think you can tell us what went on out there?"

"Well, my wife and I were parked way at the back," the man said, looking down at Luke, not noticing that the local officers were also listening intently.

"We were almost there! To the car! Wolves surrounded us. Five, six, I don't know, maybe more, too dark to tell. Bastards didn't make a sound, just kept coming at us every time we tried to move! They kept snapping at the kids legs and arms. One jumped up and just snatched the baby out of Darlene's arms! I picked up Nikki, so they went for Billie's head! I think they might have ripped off a piece of her scalp!"

"It's alright, the doctor's got her now, she'll be alright," whispered Luke. "Try and stay calm."

"John and Noele were right behind us. John must have got Noele into their car. He came back to help me. He took Nikki from me so I could grab Billie. I think someone must have put Darlene into John's car before she could try and go after the baby—I know she would have done, she was screaming with fury. Then two of the wolves went for Nikki's pant legs, trying to pull her out of John's arms.

"Then, I don't know, I think I was just about to pick Billie up when that big white one grabbed her ankle and pulled hard. I had her by the arm but I could barely hold on. Another one must have came at me from behind and grabbed my leg—not just my jeans, it had my whole leg in its mouth! I could feel it ripping though the flesh. That's when I thought we were all going to die, right there.

"But then someone, I don't know who, some big guy came in with a shovel and started swinging. He just kept trying to hit the wolves in the face to make them let go. But when others from the pack, I don't know how many, started lunging at him from behind, couldn't land many blows.

"If our neighbours hadn't stepped in then, I think we'd have all gone down. We'd have all died then! Marcus and

Carl got Nikki free and I think John, maybe, carried her back to his car. But that damn white one just wouldn't let go of Billie's ankle. It wasn't until Dougie grabbed the shovel and smashed it in the head that he released his grip—didn't seem to faze the damn thing but it did let go. I was able to back away while Dougie stood there swinging the shovel to keep it from moving back in. Then that monster started to snarl and growl at him. Man, the way it glared at Dougie, those eyes, just made my blood run cold."

"Is anyone else still out there?" interjected Hammond, as if he'd suddenly realized the attack might not be completely over.

"John, Noele, Nikki, and Darlene are still in John's car, I think," replied the man, turning to look at him. "But the baby—my son! He's gone! And where's Billie? She's bleeding so bad!"

"The doctor's got Billie, he's taking care of her in the kitchen," Luke reminded him firmly.

Just then, they all stopped at the sound of a car horn blasting just outside the emergency exit doors. Hammond ran over and pushed them open. Two men with a child between them, as well as two women, bolted up the stairs. The group scurried through the doors into the safety of the hall.

"Well, that saves us the trouble of going back out there to get them," commented Blake to Hammond.

One of the women, who was obviously Darlene, ran over to Judd, crying hysterically about the loss of her baby. Their youngest daughter Nikki, clinging to her mother, was calling frantically for her sister. Luke took the family to the kitchen where Billie was being treated. There wasn't anything he or anyone else could do about their lost baby but at least they could be together in their grief.

Hammond, Blake, and Cole took the people who had rescued Darlene and Nikki aside to see if they were injured and take statements from them.

It took more than an hour for the chaos in the hall to subside.

Luke talked to another father who'd left the meeting early with his family and who'd only avoided a similar fate to Judd's because he'd carried a flashlight. Just as he'd heard the first screams echo from across the lot where Judd and Darlene were parked, the light allowed him to spot another group of wolves near his car soon enough to make a safe retreat.

Luke calculated there must have been at least two dozen wolves on the attack that night, perhaps more. Judd's neighbours, who'd fortuitously come to his rescue, had all sustained ripped jeans and torn jacket sleeves. Luke concluded to himself that, given the circumstances, Judd and Billie were very lucky to be alive.

But that luck didn't hold.

Just before 10:30, Billie died from blood loss. An ambulance finally arrived to take her body, along with the rest of her inconsolable family, down to the hospital so that Judd's bite wounds could be sutured.

Hammond and his officers had used their squad cars to escort some of the hall's occupants to their cars in the upper parking lot. Many had simply abandoned their vehicles and caught rides home with other residents. No more incidents were reported, no more wolves were seen or heard from.

It was about this time that Luke realized he hadn't seen Jenny since the first screams began, when she'd silently disappeared from the chair beside his. When he didn't see her amongst those still milling about the hall, he headed back to the kitchen. He knew from past experience that the food hub of any community hall was a women's retreat of sorts—where they sought refuge when in need of emotional support.

He walked down the hallway just in time to see an older woman coaxing Jenny out of a large storage closet, muttering encouraging words in a soothing voice. As soon as Jenny looked up and saw Luke approaching, she dropped the old woman's protective arm and ran to him.

"I'm such a coward!" she wailed as he took her in his arms. "But as soon as I heard the screams, I just panicked. I couldn't go through all that again, couldn't see the blood and broken bodies."

"It's all right," Luke muttered soothingly, stroking her hair. "You're safe now, all the blood's been cleaned up and everyone who's been injured has been taken to hospital. Let's get you out of here."

As he guided her toward the main entrance, he noticed that the hall was almost empty. Most of the residents that had parked in the less exposed lower lot had felt safe enough to make their way out, their fear assuaged by the three armed officers now standing watch.

Luke felt Jenny stop as they crossed the threshold of the double doors and turned to look down at her. Her bright blue eyes were again brimming with tears.

"Can I stay with you tonight?" she asked, looking up into his eye beseechingly. "I don't think I can be alone."

Luke nodded silently and took her hand.

"I'm sure Pete will take care of Peg. Someone will let them know what's happened, we can be almost certain of that."

Chapter 33

"Look at me—I'm still shaking," Jenny whispered, as Luke drove his truck down the dark road into town.

"You're in shock. It was a horrible event to witness," he replied patiently.

"But I didn't even *see* anything," she wailed out loud. "I didn't even see what happened and certainly nothing happened to *me*. I didn't bleed to death or have a baby taken from my arms!"

"But you knew from the Menagerie attack what was going on outside, and that this time it involved human children rather than goats. Your mind painted pictures for you that were probably as scary as the real thing."

"YES!" she cried. "That's exactly it. As I listened to all the screaming and yelling, I could imagine what was happening in vivid detail. But I didn't *want* to see it and closing my eyes didn't help. So I looked for a place where I could barely hear what was going on. Then I just zoned out."

"I get it. No one else inside the hall really understood what was happening outside. Their ignorance protected them. But because of the attack at the farm, you knew."

"Yes, I knew those wolves were determined to snatch those children out of their parents' arms and haul them into the woods to kill them," she said bitterly.

"They only got one," Luke reminded her. "Billie didn't survive but at least they didn't get to eat her as well."

"Was her death my fault?" she asked him, her wet eyes sparkling in the glow of a street light as they drove through town. "For not telling someone sooner about the attack at the farm?"

"No, I really don't think so. In my experience, even if you'd told your story, most people wouldn't really have believed it, which means they wouldn't have taken any precautions to prevent what happened tonight."

"They will now, though. Now they've seen it with their own eyes," he added.

He saw her nod in silent agreement and sensed her discomfort as they turned onto the road to his place.

"Don't worry. It's no bother. I have a pull-out couch," Luke said patiently.

At that, he turned into the parking space nearest his trailer and held Jenny's arm as she climbed out of the truck. As he guided her through the door to the trailer, he could feel that she was indeed still trembling. She also kept furtively glancing at the wall of trees that surrounded them, as if danger hide there as well.

Blake's truck wasn't around, which didn't surprise him. She would likely be out all night dealing with the aftermath of the attack.

He settled Jenny in the kitchen booth and poured her a small glass of whiskey. She sipped at it while he silently made up the couch. He was just finishing up when he saw her visibly jump as something scratched at the door.

He went to her quickly and put his hand on her shoulder to calm her.

"It's OK. That's just Cooper, Blake's cat. He's decided that if Blake isn't home, I'm required to feed him. He doesn't take no for an answer, so I'd better let him in."

Jenny laughed a little at that as he pulled away to open the door. The big black cat strode in like he owned the place and headed for the corner of the kitchen. He stood there silently while Luke fished a half-empty can of cat food out of the fridge, dumped its contents into a dish, and slid it across the floor towards the cat.

Luke stepped back towards Jenny and asked if she needed another drink. When she shook her head no, he took her in his arms and gave her a reassuring hug.

"Will you sit out here with me until I fall asleep?" she whispered, her head on his shoulder.

"I think you might have company in that bed," he replied, nodding his head in Cooper's direction. "So don't freak out if he cuddles up with you."

She laughed lightly at that and he brushed his lips against her cheek. She turned to look into his eyes and he kissed her squarely and purposely on the lips. She sighed heavily and leaned into him, kissing him back.

After several minutes, he pulled away.

"Please don't let me sleep alone," she pleaded. "Not tonight."

He looked into her eyes for several long minutes, then took her hand. He led her into the back bedroom that held his king-sized bed and shut the door firmly behind him.

Cooper would have to sleep alone on the couch.

Chapter 34

Thursday 18 January 9:00 am

Luke and Jenny were startled awake by a loud bang and a jolt, like something big had run into the trailer.

They both sat up in bed and looked at each other quizzically.

"What the hell was that?" demanded Luke.

Luke was just starting to get out of bed when the shaking of the earthquake began.

Luke settled back and reached out for Jenny's hand as the tremours quickly increased in intensity. They could hear thumping noises elsewhere in the trailer as various objects fell, then the mirror Luke had recently installed on the back of the bathroom door smashed to the floor.

The shaking went on for almost two minutes, then just as suddenly as it had begun, it subsided.

"That was a long one!" said Jenny, with surprise. "They're usually only 10 or 20 seconds. And not nearly that strong."

"Really?" Luke remarked. "It's my first, so I have nothing to compare it to."

He quickly got out of bed and started getting dressed. As he turned, he caught sight of Jenny's perplexed face.

"Sorry," he offered, slowly buttoning his shirt, remembering that at some point during the night he had finally explained his police background in some detail.

"Occupational hazard, sort of a conditioned response to anything resembling an emergency."

He leaned over and kissed her gently.

"I didn't mean to rush off," he added

"I understand," she replied. "It'll take some getting used to, knowing you're a policeman."

As Luke opened the bedroom door to see if there had been any other damage, Cooper bolted through the door and ran under the bed. Jenny gave a quiet laugh and sat up again.

"What were you doing last night?" she asked Luke. "I woke up at one point and you weren't here. But I could hear you typing away at your laptop, so I just went back to sleep."

"I wanted to do some more research about wolf attacks before tomorrow," he replied, still standing in the doorway. "I felt like I didn't know nearly enough to be of any use to people. I hate feeling like Baylou is more knowledgeable than I am right now."

"What did you learn?" she asked.

"Nothing, really," he sighed. "I was only able to confirm what I've been told already by Rex Matterson. And Baylou."

Just then Luke heard Blake's truck pull into the driveway, so he headed outside to greet her, pulling the door firmly shut behind him. Just at that moment, the tsunami alert sirens went off.

With the wailing of the sirens in the background, Luke intercepted Blake as she slammed her truck door closed.

"What's with the sirens?" Luke demanded. "Is there really a tsunami coming?"

"Obviously, the mayor is assuming so," she replied. "But we already know quake was local, not an off-shore one. Chief says the reports he's getting indicate the chance of it generating even a small tsunami are low. He suspects that after what happened last night, the mayor doesn't didn't want to be seen failing to respond to a potential emergency.

"However, it looks like in her panic, she forgot that tsunami protocol calls for people to head to the community centre when the sirens go off! Some folks obviously aren't going to do that after the attack there last night, but many of them will—and perhaps expose themselves to another wolf attack."

Luke just shook his head in disbelief.

"I'm just here to grab some clean underwear and head back up to the hall," Blake added. "Cole's been there all night. Feel free to join us."

***

Within an hour, it was apparent that a significant tsunami for west coast communities wasn't in the cards, leaving the panic from the sirens to linger like a metallic aftertaste. But that didn't mean the earthquake hadn't delivered a significant impact to the little town as it struggled to cope with the threat from wolves.

Chapter 35

Thursday 18 January 11:00 am

The mayor called for order and prepared to address the crowd gathered in the community hall perched on the hill. There were still wet spots around the building where blood stains had been scrubbed clean, a grim reminder of the previous night's wolf attack.

While some residents had either ignored the tsunami sirens—or at least, sought higher-ground refuge elsewhere—almost two hundred brave souls were milling restlessly throughout the hall. They'd been reassured it was safe to leave their vehicles by the presence of the two armed Mounties patrolling the upper parking lot, waiting to escort drivers to the main doors. And also, by the simple fact of daylight.

As the crowd settled down, Mayor Mutts raised her hands for silence.

"I've been advised by the tsunami experts that we are in an 'all-clear' position," she began.

"It appears the earthquake we all felt this morning had an epicentre in the Mackenzie Range northeast of Ucluelet. It was a relatively shallow quake and initial estimates have been given of a Richter-scale strength of 7.9, which is stronger than we've had in a quite a few decades.

"The only significant local damage we've had is to the hospital, which is hardly surprising. As you all know, it's been long overdue for a seismic upgrade. They've had to close their doors until the damage can be assessed by engineers but luckily, there were no injuries related to the collapse.

"As soon as the storm that's paralyzed the rest of the island has subsided, we'll be air-lifting out two patients needing more advanced care who would normally have gone out by ambulance this afternoon. One patient admitted last night with severe injuries will also be taken out by air as soon as possible.

"Our first priority will be to establish a temporary emergency care centre at the library. It will be tight quarters but we think it will do for the time being. If any of you are available to help with shifting medical equipment over to the new location, it would be much appreciated—just see me or Harriet before you leave.

"The other damage is further afield but is going to have an even bigger impact on the community. Unfortunately, the quake triggered several avalanches along Highway 4, including one east of Cathedral Grove at Cameron Lake and another near Kennedy Lake. Apparently, those cliff faces—you know the ones I mean, those two spots that have been causing problems for the last decade or so—accumulated so much snow above them during this storm that the earthquake caused them to give way."

She paused as the crowd groaned and the inevitable muttering began, but she cut it short after a couple minutes.

"I know, I know! It sucks," she shouted, causing the uproar to mostly subside.

"The long and short of it is, the road is now closed and we have no idea how long it will take to get it opened but it will definitely be a while. In both cases, the avalanche also brought down loose soil and fractured rock along with the snow, which complicates the cleanup. We can't expect any immediate help from Nanaimo or Victoria with this mess, they're having their own issues with the snowstorm. So—yet again!—Tofino and Ucluelet are cut off from the outside world for the next little while, at least as far as road traffic is concerned.

"We'll arrange barge and air shipments of food and fuel but it will take a few days to get all that in place. Until then, be frugal. Ration your own supplies accordingly and share with neighbours. We missed some gas and diesel deliveries getting in just as the snowstorm hit, which means we'll have to get by with what we have on hand. I'm imposing an immediate limit of 20 litres of fuel per day for non-essential vehicles until the pumps run dry and for the foreseeable future. I know it's not much but we've been through disasters like this before. The road closure could last longer than any we've endured before but we'll manage somehow."

"What about the wolves?!" someone shouted from the audience. "Are you just not going to mention what happened here last night? Two people died!"

"Well, yes, I was getting to that. It seemed to me the earthquake damage would be top of everyone's minds," replied the mayor, trying to contain her exasperation.

"What with the earthquake this morning, we've hardly had time to process what happened last night in the upper parking lot. As far as we've been able to tell, at least two dozen wolves and perhaps more were gathered around the perimetre of the parking lot. There was one direct attack involving eight or more wolves that succeeded in pulling one child, a baby, into the forest. They severely injured another, who later died of blood loss. At least two additional incidents involving different animals were prevented by quick thinking. We have to assume these were also predatory attacks, and that if they'd been successful, more children would have been killed.

"Fortunately, that didn't happen. Sadly, Judd Burke's baby was taken by the wolves and we haven't recovered his body. His sister Billie bled to death last night as a result of her injuries before we could get her down the hill to the hospital. Judd's leg injuries are severe but he'll live. And as I said earlier, the Burkes will be air-lifted out to Victoria as soon as the weather clears to the south."

"Are you saying there's a huge pack of wolves living in the Tonquin Forest that are trying to kill and eat people?"

someone shouted from the back. "Are these the same wolves who killed those two girls at Mackenzie Beach the night before last?"

"We don't know yet," admitted the mayor, with a sigh.

"The coroner hasn't had a chance to return to Victoria but she'll go out on the same plane as the Burkes as soon as possible. However, before she leaves she'll be taking samples that will hopefully tell us if there's overlap in the events—by that I mean, if some of the same wolves were involved in both attacks.

"We won't have those results for at least a week, probably more. Victoria is at a virtual standstill because of the amount of snow that got dumped on them and it could be a week before they really get dug out from under it all. However, the coroner suspects—and its only a guess at this point—that there may be two large wolf packs operating in the area. One living in the Tonquin Forest and another perhaps in the woods behind Chesterman Beach."

"I've also had a long-overdue conversation with the wildlife officer at the Park and she has finally admitted that they've been fielding reports of increasingly aggressive wolf activity over the last few weeks, especially around the Wickaninnish Dunes. Her excuse for not sharing that information earlier was that she'd thought most of the stories of a very large pack causing trouble were not credible. She said she knew that packs traditionally operating in the Park had grown in recent years and had split off at least one pack that's been living in the Tonquin Forest. But the existence of a pack consisting of dozens of animals suddenly operating within the Park made no logical sense to her."

Luke stood up then and prepared to share the information he'd been hoarding. He might not be believed but sensed the time was right.

"Most of you don't know me, but I'm a wildlife safety specialist and have worked for the RCMP around the country in that capacity for more than a decade," he began after introducing himself.

"My job is to assist communities dealing with particularly contentious wildlife problems, especially those that involve predators. I'm currently on leave and therefore not here in an official capacity. I came to Tofino with the intension of making it my home and have taken an interest in the recent wolf attacks because—like all of you here—I want to feel safe in my community.

"That said, I have a lot of experience dealing with problems like you're having, including interviewing people who have witnessed odd wildlife behaviour and talking to victims of predatory animal attacks. I quickly get a sense of when information is credible, and what's been blown out of proportion by fear or imagination.

"I'm here to say that over the last few weeks, I've had several conversations with your neighbour Baylou. I know many of you have your doubts about her but I've found her to be quite sober, lucid, and a keen observer of details.

"To make a long story short, Baylou has been noticing unusual wolf activity since early December, when her dog was killed by a wolf. Her opinion is that the deep snow in the mountains this winter has pushed several packs of interior wolves west toward the coast looking for food. She believes several of these interior packs have joined together as they moved west and that when they got here, they either killed off wolves in the local packs, or incorporated them into their group, taking over their territory.

"Biologists call these large groups of wolves 'superpacks' and what I've learned is that they almost always form under conditions of food stress. It means what Baylou has surmised about what's been happening around town seems to fit what scientists know about how wolves sometimes adapt to lack of readily-available food.

"Baylou based her conclusions on changes in howling patterns she's heard around town and near her cabin, and from talking with local First Nations individuals. Apparently, there have been a marked increase in attacks by wolves on dogs and even some on children, among other incidents, at Opitsat and other reserves in the area, incidents you probably haven't been hearing about.

"Also, over the last several weeks, there have been several attacks by wolves on some of the animals housed at the Menagerie just outside of town, the place operated by the Marcuses. The last of these attacks involved a very large pack of at least two dozen wolves, which Baylou and the owners witnessed first-hand. That happened almost a week ago. I only heard about those incidents the day before yesterday and there hasn't really been an opportunity to share that information, what with all that's been going on.

"That's unfortunate. But now we have the opportunity to put all of these pieces of the puzzle together, and that's the first step in finding a solution. It's not my place to take over the management of this crisis from the mayor or Sergeant Hammond, I can only offer my professional opinion and advice.

"However, we have to do *something*. If there are indeed one very large superpack of wolves actively hunting in the area, we have a big problem. Because last night's attack, and the one at Mackenzie beach the night before, prove that these wolves now consider people to be acceptable prey. And while its true that wolves don't usually attack people, we are dealing with unusual circumstances here. The natural reticence wolves have for attacking humans has broken down in these animals and all of us are now at risk. Keeping people safe has to be our first priority."

"Are you saying these attacks have been going on for six weeks or more without anyone saying anything to me?" asked the mayor, her voice rising in anger.

"Yes, that's unfortunately true," Luke replied, a bit defensively. "But I think everyone involved has been having trouble putting these incidents into the context of what they knew—or thought they knew—about wolf behaviour, as well as worrying they might not be believed if they said anything."

The mayor just huffed and shook her head in frustration as the agitation of the crowd increased.

"But what are we going to do about these wolves—just shoot them all?" shouted someone from behind Luke. "No one here even owns guns anymore!"

"Please, all of you sit down and relax for a few minutes, maybe have a cup of coffee while I talk to the mayor and Sergeant Hammond," Luke responded in a soothing voice, hoping to placate the crowd.

"The quicker we come up with a workable plan, the safer we'll all be," he added.

Chapter 36

The crowd gathered at the hall was getting decidedly restless again. Despite Luke's warning, more than half of them had left since the mayor had spoken that morning, fortunately without any more wolf confrontations in the parking lot. The mayor was now preparing to address the group after more than an hour of furious consultation with Luke and Sergeant Hammond.

They hadn't really come up with a plan but the mayor knew she couldn't hold the crowd off much longer. She'd managed to get Chelsea Kettle from the Park on the phone for a consultation but all the wildlife officer could suggest was that everyone go home and stay there until all community stakeholders could sit down and put together a viable plan to deal with the wolf threat.

The mayor simply rolled her eyes at the two men as she ended her call with Kettle.

"I think the problem is that none of us, myself included, have ever dealt with a predator like wolves before," Luke stated. "Cougars, black bears, and even polar bears are all lone hunters—all you have to do is track down a single animal at a time. But dozens of wolves working together to target the same prey is an entirely different threat. It's

221

my professional opinion that at the very least, we need both more experienced man-power, as well as more fire-power, than is currently at our disposal."

"But how are we going to get that, with the road out of town cut off—and government higher-ups elsewhere on the island dealing with their own problems?" asked the mayor.

"It seems to me we're on our own, at least for a few days," she added. "My understanding is that because they're closer, first responders out of Ucluelet have been called out to deal with the disaster on the highway at Kennedy Lake. They've pulled most of the heavy equipment available out to the avalanche site, along with all the able-bodied residents willing to assist. Bob and I have tried calling for backup support to be flown in as soon as possible from Victoria. But even when flights resume, I get the feeling we've been put at the bottom of the list."

"I really wonder if it's more than that," said Luke with restraint, turning to look over at Hammond. "Perhaps you aren't being taken seriously because none of your supervisors believes that what you're telling them could possibly be true,"

"Yeah, there's also that," replied Hammond with a sigh.

***

What these three weren't aware of, but perhaps should have anticipated, was that someone in the crowd the previous night had called Uncle Jack on the reserve at Opitsat and told him of the parking lot wolf attacks.

That information accelerated a plan that had been taking shape over the last two weeks under Uncle Jack's tutelage. Suddenly, a rescue mission was set in motion that did not involve any of the community leaders struggling for a solution at the town hall.

Chapter 37

Thursday 18 January 3:00 pm

Once the initial panic over the earthquake had passed that morning, a group of First Nations hunters with rifles set sail on a fishing boat from Opitsat. They were greeted at the dock by a group of hunting friends and relatives from Tofino, waiting patiently in their trucks for the boat to arrive.

The hunters from Opitsat were scooped up, and the convoy of trucks moved silently and largely unnoticed out of town. They had a mission to implement that night which they weren't prepared to share with anyone. Their task was bigger than anything they'd ever even contemplated before. Calls to specific people had gone out up and down the coast to trusted hunters and they had been secretly coming together in Tofino over the last week.

Their weapons were almost as varied in shape and size as the men themselves. Most of the rifles were the ancient models preferred by subsistence hunters, supplemented by a variety of modern scopes and night-vision capabilities. A few hunters had more modern fire-power, including styles of weapons made illegal by recent government legislation, which had been obtained through black market means for just such an emergency.

Unbeknownst to him, Luke's revelations at the hall that morning had also been relayed to Uncle Jack. When passed along to the hunters, it only solidified their resolve. Something had to be done, and quickly.

Most Tofino residents had not even contemplated what they might prepare for dinner that night when the critical mission began. Simultaneously, the hunters moved through the forest and planted their live bait in three strategic locations—pairs of tethered goats, muzzled for the time being.

As the hour of dusk approached, the snipers slipped the silencers from the goats and hid themselves in the trees nearby.

And then they waited.

Waited for the bleating of the goats and the failing light to attract predators unable to resist an easy meal.

When the packs moved in to kill, the hunters responded. They had to be quick and remember their targets. Some were assigned to take out the front-line attackers, others were to pick off those waiting in the shadows.

Some were always waiting in the shadows.

They would only get one chance. They had to kill as many pack members as possible, as quickly as possible, before they scattered into the forest.

The best hunter of them all was assigned a special task. His job was to kill the ghostly white alpha leader of the largest pack and retrieve the carcass. Their people needed to see with their own eyes that this devil had been eliminated—so many had seen or heard about the actions of the big male at Opitsat that it had become legend.

The chosen hunter had appointed two others to stand with him, to ensure the job was done. What if his rifle jammed? Or he slipped and fell at the wrong moment? Or he simply couldn't get a clear shot?

He could not afford to fail, for any reason. He could not be so proud to go alone to do this important job.

Chapter 38

Friday 19 January 9:00 am

Jenny was still sleeping when Luke took the call from Hammond, who'd been relayed a cryptic message from an anonymous caller to dispatch earlier that morning.

"Apparently, the man simply said, 'They've been put in their place. Thank Uncle Jack'," explained the Sergeant.

"Did he mean the wolves?" asked Luke.

"I presume so. I can't think what else it would mean."

"What have they done?"

"I don't know but I'll call you back if I find out. Someone must know what's happened," replied Hammond, ending the call abruptly.

Luke stared out the window at Blake's truck parked in its usual spot, realizing he hadn't really talked to her in days. Then his thoughts turned to Baylou, and he suddenly realized he might find the answers at the beach.

He was startled out of his thoughts by Jenny appearing in the doorway of the bedroom.

"What is it? Has something else happened?" she asked in a quiet, fearful voice.

"I'm not sure but I think I can find out. And you should come with me. How fast can you get dressed?"

"Give me two minutes," she replied resolutely, already turning back towards the bedroom.

He told himself he shouldn't really expect Baylou would be on the beach this morning, yet he had a gut feeling that's exactly where she would be.

And she'd be waiting to tell him what had happened.

***

"I hope she isn't spooked by having you here me but I think you need to hear what she has to say," explained Luke as the two walked along the sand towards the tombolo at the south end.

Wind was howling off the dark water in powerful gusts and enormous waves were pounding ashore, leaving only a small protected area behind the pseudo-island up ahead.

He thought that's where Baylou would wait and he was right.

However, just as Luke and Jenny approached the lee of the rocky mass, Luke saw the back of Baylou, pushing her bike along the sand, headed away from them.

"Wait here," he told Jenny, dropping her hand.

He took off in an awkward run across the damp sand. Surprised at how far she'd gotten in such a short amount of time, once he reached Baylou he was panting slightly with exertion.

"Please don't go," he pleaded with her, as she continued walking, her back to him.

"I realize you don't know her but she works at the Menagerie. Her name is Jenny and she saw the same attack on the goats that you did, and also the ones before that. She knows what you've been saying about the wolves is true. You can trust her."

Baylou stopped and turned around. After staring at him for several long minutes, she began walking back towards him.

They walked along together in silence for a few paces, then Baylou stopped and looked over at him.

"Someone I know, long ago,"

"Who, Jenny?" he asked, decidedly perplexed.

"Hair and eyes, those eyes," she replied. "It was a long time ago."

Luke just shook his head as Baylou resumed walking towards the spot Jenny now stood waiting. When they were all face-to-face, Luke began without preamble.

"Do you know what happened last night? Bob Hammond got a call from someone saying the wolves had been 'put in their place'. Do you know what that means?"

Baylou had been staring intently at Jenny, but abruptly shifted her gaze at Luke while she answered.

"Hunters killed them. Had to, needed to put things right," she said calmly.

"Uncle Jack told everyone that, at the meeting— shouldn't come as a surprise," she added, turning again to stare at Jenny.

"You look like a ghost," she muttered, her words barely audible over the wind.

Shaking her head in fear or confusion—Luke couldn't tell which—Baylou again set off along the beach. But soon she turned to have the last word.

"Survivors will leave," she shouted. "Most of them. They know they're not wanted here."

Chapter 39

Friday 19 January 11:00 am

Luke made a quick call to let Hammond know what he'd learned from Baylou and then dropped Jenny off at the Menagerie, having successfully reassured her that she'd be safe there. She hadn't been looking forward to talking to Peg after the way she'd abandoned her over the last two days but knew it couldn't be avoided.

Her parting words to him had been, "I just have to do it."

Heading home, he realized there was something he needed to do as well, which he also didn't relish. He didn't know if Blake realized that Jenny had been spending nights with him or not. But even if she only suspected, he knew she should hear it from him before any more time passed.

As he pulled into his parking spot on their shared acreage, he groaned inwardly at the sight of Blake's truck, which he'd secretly hoped would have been gone by now. Shaking his head at his own cowardice, he headed directly over to her trailer.

"Too late for coffee?" he asked, opening the door after a perfunctory knock.

"I guess not," she called out, from the bedroom. "I'll be right out."

Luke poured himself a cup of coffee from the carafe on the counter.

"It feels like ages since I saw you," Blake stated accusingly, as she walked into the room, wet hair dripping onto her shirt. "Where the hell have you been?"

"Just trying to make sense of what's been happening, like everyone else," he countered.

"I've also been spending time with Jenny, who works at the Menagerie," he added. "It turns out she witnessed the wolf attack that happened there last week—the one I told you all about yesterday. The attack at the community hall really got her spooked, and she was afraid to go back to Peg's, so I took her home. She's been kind of hanging out with me ever since."

"Days *and* nights?" Blake queried, raising an eyebrow, although without the smiling face he was used to seeing when she teased him.

Luke took a sip of his coffee. Trying to lighten the mood, gave her a sheepish grin before nodding his head yes.

"What can I say? I think she's great," he admitted. "Sweet, but smart. Capable, and beautiful. I think I'm really falling for her."

"She's a little young, isn't she?" Blake asked, unable to quell her innate female cattiness.

"She's older than she looks. And ten years isn't that big a difference at our age," he retorted, more defensively than he might have intended.

"It's alright, Luke," Blake responded, after a minute-long staring match.

She turned her back on him, and added, "You don't owe me an explanation."

"Well, 'owe' may be too strong a word," he replied pragmatically. "But I wanted you to know. I never meant to hurt you. After Christmas, I mean."

"Christmas was about not being alone, nothing more," she said, shrugging her shoulders. "I never expected it meant we were getting back together. Did you?"

"I don't know, maybe," he muttered. "But then I met Jenny and I suddenly felt strong enough to try for another serious relationship. You and I just never seem to be able to make it work over the long-term. We just end up hurting each other. I didn't want to go through that again."

"Yeah, I know," Blake said quietly, turning and putting her hand on his arm. "It's probably for the best for us to just be friends."

"Are you sure?" he said, searching her face for signs she was braving her way through an emotional lie.

"Yeah, I'm sure," she replied, turning away again. "I admit I had a fleeting hope what went on between us might have been a new beginning. But deep down, I think I knew it was probably a fantasy. I'll get over it."

Luke reached over and spun her around, taking her in his arms for a friendly bear-hug. She laughed out loud as he squeezed her extra tight, then let her go.

"I don't want to lose you again," he said earnestly. "Whatever else happens, I need you in my life. As my best friend."

"Me too," she said lightly, reaching up to brush her lips against his left cheek before pulling away.

"Now tell me, where were you and your girl off to this morning?" she demanded, holding him an arms-length away. "I saw you rush off out of here before I'd even put the coffee on."

She motioned him toward the kitchen booth as she poured herself a cup of coffee.

They spent the next hour or so in amicable chatter. Luke filled her in on what Baylou had said on the beach and added some details from Jenny about the Menagerie attack. Blake told him she'd just heard that the results on the samples the coroner had collected from the Mackenzie Beach Resort attack had come in.

"They confirmed several of the same wolf pack members had also been involved in whatever had happened to the two boys whose gear I found at the campground," she said. "DNA left on several scraps of clothing that searchers found at the edge of the road near the campsite confirm the boys had been attacked by wolves and dragged into the woods."

"Do you know yet who they were?" asked Luke.

"Yeah, we do. Someone took their packs apart and found one of them had a wallet at the bottom. These kids had been reported missing over a week ago. But as far as I know, their families haven't yet been notified."

"I can't for the life of me understand why Hammond is dragging his feet on that," Luke said with more than a hint of sarcasm.

Chapter 40

Friday 19 January 1:00 pm

While Luke talked to Blake, Jenny had spent the last two hours telling Peg what she'd been up to.

"Don't worry about it, I understand why you were too afraid to come back to the farm after what happened at the hall," Peg conceded. "Unfortunately, I can indeed imagine how horrific it must have been.

"And as you know, Pete had come up to the house to stay with me while you went to the meeting," she continued. "He just stayed and slept on the couch when you didn't come home. One of my friends called me just before midnight to tell me what had happened at the meeting and that she'd seen you leave with Luke. So, I actually knew you were safe."

"Thank you, Peg—that means a lot," Jenny said with relief.

"Right now I'm more concerned that Ian hasn't been able to get home," Peg replied. "After I finally told him about the attack on the goats, he'd insisted on coming home. But he still had a few more days work to do, and then between the snowstorm and the earthquake, it looks like he'll be unable to get here for days. Well, you know why—priorities are being given for medical and fuel transport. It looks like he'll have to wait for a flight to Port Alberni and charter a boat from there."

"Ian says to keep the goats in the shed until he gets back, Peg added. "He knows they won't like it but says at least they'll be safe. Same for the horses and donkeys. He says he's already bought two hunting rifles, one for himself and one for Pete."

"Well, I don't know if that's really necessary—Baylou seems to think the wolves are gone," Jenny replied. "I know you don't really trust her but she seemed genuinely convinced the wolves are no longer a threat. We don't know exactly what happened last night but Luke thinks she knows and is simply not saying."

"Well, I don't think Ian will believe the threat's over until he sees it with his own eyes. And now he's afraid the twins will come early and I won't be able to get help if I need it, what with the hospital out of commission. He tried to talk me into requesting a medical evacuation to Victoria as soon as it's possible to fly. I told him I'd go if he insisted but that I wouldn't budge before he gets home. Even if you can't stay here with me, I'm not leaving without him."

"After what happened to the goats, I felt so overwhelmed with fear during the wolf attack at the hall," Jenny said, unable to keep the guilt out of her voice. "Being with Luke just made me feel so safe. But it was unfair of me to trade my own safety for yours when you've been feeling so vulnerable. I know I'd promised to stay with you and from now on, I will."

Jenny reached out and gave Peg a big hug, not sure how she'd summon up the gumption to fulfill this rash promise.

"I'm really not sure where things are going with Luke. A romantic relationship with him may not be what I need right now," she added with false bravado. "Sleeping with him may have been a bad idea. I should probably let things cool down, see how things go. He's busy making friends with Baylou anyway, but she kind of gives me the creeps."

"What do you mean by that?" asked Peg. "I thought you trusted her."

"*Luke* trusts her," Jenny replied. "I don't know her at all. But when Luke took me to meet her, she just stared at me, said I looked like a ghost. The look on her face gave me goosebumps. Luke says Baylou can be rudely frank and also secretive, that it's just her nature. But he doesn't really know her either, he just met her a few weeks ago."

"I bet you just remind her of someone from her past," said Peg soothingly. "They say everyone has a double out there somewhere—maybe your double crossed paths with Baylou at some point."

"Maybe, but the constant staring really unnerved me," Jenny replied, visibly shivering. "She really creeped me out."

Chapter 41

Friday 19 January 4:00 pm

The boat from Tofino sputtered into the dock at Opitsat just before dusk. On board were the hunters who had taken care of Tofino's wolf problem, as well as their prize.

It took four strong men to unload the carcass of the pale-coloured wolf onto the dock and transport it to Uncle Jack's cabin down the beach. Children watched from the windows of their houses, knowing better than to try and follow the solemn procession on foot.

The men laid the body of the white beast at the foot of the steps as the elder opened his front door. One of the hunters stepped forward with a bulging skin bag and poured the contents out beside the wolf's head. The big canine teeth tinkled as they fell to the ground, making an impressively large pile.

"You've done well," said the old man. "And the rest?"

"We got most of them. A few got away but we expected that. Crew took the bodies out behind Ucluelet and buried them with a backhoe. Too many to burn."

"The survivors will leave of their own accord—they will understand our message," replied Uncle Jack, descending the stairs to stand by the slain pack leader.

"We will honour them with a ceremony when the time is right. I will dance as our ancestors have done before me, to renew our alliance."

Uncle Jack then appointed two of his closest allies to stand beside him. He whispered instructions to them on the special rituals and chants they must use in the process of preparing the skin, previously known only to himself.

He told them he would dance while wearing this sacredly-prepared skin of the wolf leader and a belt adorned with the canine teeth taken from the other pack members before their burial. He would practice this dance to perfection in total secrecy, as its performance would be necessary to rekindle the recently soured relationship between his people and the wolf.

He motioned for one of the youngest men to step forward with his phone to take a picture of the white wolf's carcass.

"Only this one shall be shared," he proclaimed with quiet authority, pointing to the photo he was shown.

And so, in the following months only that one photo would make its way into the newspapers.

Although a few other photos had been taken of the triumphant aftermath of the hunt, they were closely guarded by the community as evidence of their victory.

Chapter 42

Saturday 20 January 9:00 am

Luke had again found Baylou on the beach.

"Howling stopped," declared Baylou, staring out to sea.

"Gone," she added after a long pause. "Most, anyway. Back to the mountains, to find more food."

"It's only been one day," noted Luke. "How can you be sure they've left?"

"Wolves aren't fools. They learned their lesson. If they were still here, feeling like fighting back, they'd be telling each other how clever they've been. Wouldn't be able to help themselves. I'd have heard them."

"Wolves gloat?" asked Luke incredulously.

"Oh yes. At least, bold ones do. One's that stay aren't bold."

"Will they come back?"

"Not these ones. Other's will, eventually. But they will tread more carefully. More respectful. Because of what happened."

"I hope you're right," replied Luke with conviction.

Baylou just looked at him, pale eyebrows raised. Luke smiled back at her and shrugged his shoulders in apology.

After a few minutes of silence, Luke got up the nerve to ask Baylou what he really wanted to know.

"I have a question," he said plainly. "It's personal, so you may choose not to answer. But I'm curious about your reaction to meeting Jenny yesterday. Have you met her before?"

"Long ago, when she was born. Spitting image of her father."

"What are you saying? You were there when she was born? You knew her father?"

Baylou turned to him then, her voice barely rising above the sound of the waves.

"She is the daughter of Mingo. I called her Raven. They took her away. Never saw her again. Like I said, a ghost."

With that, the old woman turned and pushed her bike away from Luke along the wet sand. As he watched her figure recede into the distance along the beach, he wondered what Jenny would think of this exchange.

He didn't have to wait long to find out, as he'd arranged to meet Jenny for lunch. She'd been reluctant to leave Peg again so soon but he promised he'd take her back to the farm as soon as they were done.

"This question may seem odd, but are you by any chance adopted?" he asked her gently, over coffee when they'd finished eating.

"Yes, but why would you ask?" she replied. "It's not something I hide but some people wrongly assume I must be a broken person because of it, so I don't go around announcing it."

"Well, I had an interesting conversation with Baylou this morning. From what I can deduce from her cryptic response to my question, it appears that the reason she said you looked like a ghost is that she gave birth to a daughter many years ago that she must have been forced to give up for adoption. She said you look exactly like that baby's father, whose name was Mingo. She said she'd named the baby Raven."

Jenny abruptly sat back in her chair and stared at him.

"Riley is my middle name," she whispered. "My mother said that Raven was the only name listed on my original birth certificate. She said it sounded odd to her as a legal name, so she chose something similar to replace it with. But she told me why she'd done it, so I would know. But I've never told anyone. I think of it as a private name."

Then she told him about finding out she'd been born in Port Alberni and being drawn to spend time on the west coast.

"I wasn't really looking for my birth mother when I came here," she said. "Only for some sense of connection to my ancestral roots in general."

Luke took her hands in his across the table and smiled.

"I think Baylou may be your birth mother," he whispered.

Chapter 43

Saturday 20 January, 3:00 pm

Luke had taken Jenny back to Peg's as he'd promised, even though he hated to do so, given the shock she'd just had. But he figured she'd need some time to digest the information before she could even think about doing anything about it, like confronting Baylou.

How would Baylou take the news, he wondered? After all this time?

His thoughts were interrupted by a brief knock on the door, which opened almost immediately. Blake poked her head in.

"Want to come with me into the station?" she asked in a rush. "I'd say it's time we got some answers on what's happened with the wolves."

"Yeah, I quite agree," he answered, grabbing his coat. As he pulled on boots at the door, he fished for more information.

"Why the rush? Have you heard something?"

"Apparently someone sent a photo of a dead wolf to Hammond," she replied as they both headed for her truck.

As she drove into the detachment, Blake relayed her other news.

"Also, it seems we might have another suspicious death tied to these wolves. We got an inquiry about two young men who headed this way to surf just before the road closed because of the snowstorm, but haven't been heard from since. When we started digging, we found out their van was recovered in the impound lot, towed from the Long Beach parking lot the day of the town meeting on the Mitch Rodgers attack. And yesterday, someone turned in two badly-battered surfboards that washed up on Third Beach to one of the surf shops. The boys' mother has identified the boards as theirs.

"We don't know what happened to these kids, but it's possible the wolves got them, especially if they were surfing at dusk or dawn with no one else around. It can be damn isolated out there this time of year—more so with the roads closed. Damn but kids can be stupid sometimes! Like those kids camping where no one could see them."

She and Luke both shook their heads sadly at the folly of youth, remembering the remains of the camping gear Blake had found just a few days earlier off Mackenzie Beach.

As Blake turned to pull into the parking lot, Luke noticed the mayor and her assistant disappearing through the front doors of the detachment.

"I guess we're just in time," sniped Blake as they exited the truck, remembering why they were here.

Hammond's small office was filled with people, including Mayor Mutts, several town councillors, and

Chelsea Kettle, the wildlife conservation officer from the Park. There was a loud argument going on, clearly driven by the Parks official.

"I'll tell you what happened," she shouted. "They've all been killed! Opitsat hunters organized an ambush and just slaughtered all the wolf packs overnight!"

"You don't know that!" replied Hammond. "You're assuming based on one photo and a cryptic message."

"What other conclusion am I supposed to come to, under the circumstances?" she countered. "You saw the picture. Where do you think all those wolf canines came from, except from other wolves that were killed? You don't think that was part of the message? They're proud of what they did! And what about the wolves that survived, if any even did? What do they do now that their entire pack structure has been destroyed?"

"You don't have to keep shouting," replied the mayor, her voice also raised above its normal timbre. "I understand that you're angry the wolves were killed but your plan that people simply stay indoors until the threat passed was probably not realistic, even if I agreed with you at the time."

Luke and Blake had positioned themselves in the doorway, and now Luke took a step forward. He let out a loud whistle to get everyone's attention, then turned to the very angry woman in the Parks Canada uniform.

"Chelsea, it had to be done," he said in his most conciliatory voice. "I think you know that, in your heart. Locking people up to keep them safe until the wolves went away was never a workable strategy. Folks have had their fill of that as a solution to anything.

"And really, you can't have spent the last decade promoting indigenous values about living with wolves and then complain when Uncle Jack comes up with a quick resolution to an extremely dangerous situation. It's been a problem for him and his people as well as for us, don't forget. He just didn't see a need to ask for permission."

"How can you say that?" she shouted back at him. "Since when is killing dozens of wolves part of traditional indigenous values?"

"Actually, he told you when—at the town meeting. He was trying to say that there are indigenous rules that apply when exceptional wolf behaviour occurs, which sometimes happens. You just didn't listen carefully enough. And just because you were never told when you entered into your wolf partnership with First Nations that exceptions could happen—or that very different rules might apply when they did—that's not Uncle Jack's fault. You simply didn't ask the right questions. Perhaps you didn't ask any questions at all."

"Oh, for fucks sake!" she ranted. "I can't believe you of all people are defending what they did!"

"I've talked to Baylou," Luke continued as if she hadn't interrupted. "She's better informed than any of you about what's been going on, and all her instincts so far have been spot on. She told me most of the remaining pack members will scatter east, and may eventually head back into the mountains. Perhaps a few might stay, but they won't be willing or able to launch the kind of attacks that the larger packs were doing. They'll be laying low for a long time and sticking to natural prey."

"The threat of more attacks has been neutralized," added Blake. "I think most of you are just mad because you had absolutely no part in fixing this disaster and didn't know about it until it was on top of you."

"It's against the law to kill wolves in the Park," stated Chelsea resolutely, as if no one else had spoken. "I'll prosecute them all."

"Really?" demanded Luke. "Where's the crime scene, the evidence? You have a single photo with no provenience, no bodies, and no witnesses."

"Give it a rest, Chelsea," the mayor said wearily. "We'll tell the public the alpha wolf of the pack was unfortunately killed in response to an attack, providing the photo as proof, and say that the others have left the area as a result. We don't have to say how many wolves we think were involved—that won't serve any purpose except to spread fear. We'll tell people to keep their pets close for a week or so and then call an all-clear.

"We'll have enough trouble on our hands with the road closure and the hospital being out of commission. People will forget. Most of the people who died were not locals. Even if we tried, it's unlikely the investigations into their deaths will move forward with any speed. There's just too much else going on. And it's my guess the Burkes will not want to stay in Tofino after losing their two children. A sizable settlement to help them set up elsewhere might go a long way towards encouraging them to put the entire grizzly incident behind them while they grieve. "

"So, we just sweep it all under the rug?" Chelsea demanded. "Not just the human deaths, but we pretend the illegal slaughter of wolf packs never happened?"

"Yes," replied Luke. "Because if you acknowledge the human deaths you also have to acknowledge the viciousness and lethality of the wolf attacks, both of which run counter to the narrative of wolf behaviour you've been repeating for more than a decade. If you want to salvage anything out of this crisis for your conservation program, you'll have to come to terms with that.

"Or, you can do what Uncle Jack suggests he's willing to do—wait to see if the wolves repopulate and see how they behave. This is just my opinion, but you might want to consider that the Park might not be a good place for wolves to live anymore—that you'd be doing them and yourselves a favour if you simply drive off any that try to repopulate, before they even get settled in. Because it seems to me that for too long, you've been ignoring the fact that when wolves start attacking dogs, it means they're too food stressed to be living in harmony with people."

Luke shook his head when the yelling simply resumed after he'd finished speaking, and turned to Blake.

"Do you really want to stay and hear more of this?" he asked Blake in a tired voice.

"No, let's just go," she replied. "I'm not sure any decision will be made today anyway, not with tempers this high."

Back in the parking lot, as Blake started her truck, she turned to Luke.

"Where to, then? Home?"

"Yeah, I need to pick up my truck. I want to check on Jenny."

Blake raised her eyebrows at him briefly, then shrugged her acceptance as she turned out of the parking lot.

"You know, I just realized something kind of odd," he said before they'd gone very far.

"What's that?" she replied. "That you're not sure you want to live here anymore?"

"No, not that. It just occurred to me that during this entire crisis, I never once saw a wolf," he said with some awe in his voice.

"I don't think that's ever happened before," he added. "I was only peripherally involved with the management of this crisis, which is understandable since I wasn't here in any official capacity. But it's still odd that I didn't actually have to deal with any of the animals themselves. To the extent that I never even saw one of these wolves, even from afar. Just a few tracks."

"Is that really significant?" Blake responded.

"Well, yeah, I think so. It means that what I enjoyed most about these last few weeks was figuring out the people part of the problem, the gathering of information. It was less about addressing attacking animals head-on and more about understanding who was going to come up with the solution and why. Or something like that."

"Like doing the work of a police detective, you mean?" Blake replied, not working very hard to keep the mocking tone out of her voice.

"Yeah, I guess it sounds kind of stupid when I say it out loud but that's it, really. I know that technically speaking I've always been a police officer first but I always thought my tracking and hunting skills were the most critical part of my success in this specialty. And maybe they were, most of the time. But being on the sidelines of this crisis has shown me that I've not only become better at the background part of the work than I realized, but I think I like it more than simply hunting down misbehaving animals."

"So, what are you going to do about it?" replied Blake. "Come back to work and take the detective's exam?"

"I don't think so. I'm still not sure I want to be part of this organization anymore. I found I liked not having to follow orders and protocol these last few weeks."

"So I've noticed. And I'll admit I've been a bit jealous of that, I think I may be just as far along the dissatisfaction curve as you are with this job. But I've also noticed you've hardly taken any photographs lately. Hard to make a success of a new business with that approach. How do you expect to make a living as a photographer if you don't take any pictures?"

"I'll have to do some thinking on that," admitted Luke as Blake nosed her big truck into her home parking space.

"And what about that girl?" she added.

"That too," he said softly, leaning over to kiss her cheek before jumping out and heading over to his own vehicle.

Chapter 44

Saturday 20 January 6:00 pm

It was fully dark but bright outside spotlights illuminated the farmyard of the Menagerie as Luke pulled his truck up next to the house.

He hadn't called first, so was contrite when Jenny appeared at the back door, fear on her face.

"What's wrong?" she cried out from the doorway. "What's happened?"

"Sorry, I didn't mean to frighten you," he called out as he walked toward her. "Nothing's wrong, I just wanted to see you. Check you were alright."

She fell into his arms as soon as his feet hit the landing and he held her for several long minutes.

Luke pulled away to take his suddenly ringing phone out of his pocket. The call was from Blake.

"Sorry," Blake began. "Didn't mean to interrupt your evening. But I just got a call from Cole to say he'd just picked up Baylou from the side of the highway and taken her to the temporary hospital. It looks like she had a heart attack. I thought you'd want to know."

"Thanks," replied Luke curtly, ending the call abruptly.

"What is it?" asked Jenny, searching his face for clues.

"It looks like Baylou has suffered a heart attack. I should go, but do you want to come with me? I know you haven't had much time to process the news that she may be your birth mother, but you may not have another chance to find out for sure."

Without a word, Jenny turned back into the mud room. She emerged a minute later with her boots on and a coat in hand. Luke helped her slip on the short jacket and took her hand as he headed towards his truck.

The mood during the short ride to the library was sombre. Neither said a word. Luke swerved into the nearest parking slot without much regard for the barely-visible boundary lines, and Jenny didn't wait for him to come around and open her door as she normally would have done.

Once inside the makeshift hospital, they were shown to the area where Baylou's gurney had been parked. It wasn't at all private but the expected monitors and support hoses were being overseen by a nurse, who was at that moment taking her blood pressure.

"Is she conscious?" asked Luke in a subdued voice.

"She's in and out," replied the nurse in a hushed tone. "It looks bad, the doctor's not sure she'll survive this one."

"She's had other heart attacks?" Jenny inquired.

"Two that we know about," said the nurse. "Both times, like today, she was brought in because she collapsed in public. There could well have been others. She's always refused surgery and I doubt she takes the medication we've given her, stubborn old coot. And she's never given us a next-of-kin to notify, insists she has no family."

"Is it alright if we try and talk to her, then? Just for a few minutes?" asked Luke.

"You're the wildlife Mountie guy from the meeting, aren't you?" asked the nurse. "You've befriended her?"

"Yes, that's right," Luke admitted.

"Go ahead, then, see if she comes around. As I said, the doctor is not very hopeful she'll come through. But it might make her more comfortable, seeing a friendly face. Just don't stay too long."

Surprised that his earlier public statements appeared to give him some kind of preferred status with the nurse, Luke took her place beside the bed next to Baylou and Jenny moved in close to him. He took Baylou's frail hand in his and rubbed the back of it with his thumb.

Baylou slowly opened her eyes and she looked around until her gaze fell on Luke's face.

"Handsome one!" she whispered. "Come to say goodbye?"

"I hope this isn't a final goodbye," insisted Luke, his eyes tearing up.

"I brought Jenny back to see you, she has something to tell you," he added, hooking an arm around Jenny and guiding her into his place next to the bed.

"I was born in 1993 in Port Alberni. I was adopted. The only name on my birth certificate was 'Raven', given to me by my birth mother. Was that you?"

"Ah, '93. The war, the jail. Mingo left, no more beach shack. Then Raven. You have her eyes. And the hair! Just like her father," muttered Baylou. "Beautiful baby, Raven—I said goodbye long ago. All grown up now."

Baylou became agitated then, looking around the room.

"Where is he? Where's he gone?" she croaked.

Luke stepped over to take her hand again and she settled back on her pillow. Jenny's eyes filled with tears.

"Tell Willie goodbye," whispered Baylou, gasping for breath. "Such a good boy, he'll be alright."

"I will," replied Luke, squeezing her hand gently.

And with that, she was gone—simply closed her eyes, exhaled one last time, and went limp. The monitor alarms went off, which the nurse quickly silenced. Without a word, she pointed to the Do Not Resuscitate sign taped to it and shrugged her shoulders.

"I'm guessing that's not quite the acknowledgement you expected," Luke said soothingly as he took Jenny into his arms.

Jenny sobbed almost soundlessly for a few minutes and then turned her head up to look at him.

"I don't know. I think I got as much confirmation as I had any right to expect, given the circumstances. She only knew me as a newborn, for a few hours at most. I'm not sure if she was remembering me or my father, to be honest."

"It sounds like she really loved him, if that's any consolation," said Luke.

"I think it is. Coming out of love is better than not, I'd say. I've always felt at home here and knowing Baylou has been here all along maybe explains why. Conceived in a beach shack, from the sounds of it. What war was there in 1993?"

"Betsy says it was called 'The War in the Woods,' a conservation fight over commercial logging," replied Luke.

"So I'm both a war baby and a beach baby," said Jenny with a smile. "Who would have ever guessed that?"

"Is that enough?" asked Luke gently.

"Yeah, I think so," Jenny replied, squeezing his hand.

"Let's get you back to Peg's," said Luke. "I'll have to see if I can find Willie tomorrow. His family may want to arrange a funeral. It sounded to me like she was closer to them than anyone else around here and if anyone deserves that honour, they do."

Chapter 45

Sunday 21 January 8:00 am

Luke was not optimistic that he'd find Willie on the beach this early but saw him up ahead on the perch he'd found him on weeks earlier, staring out to sea.

It was obvious when he got up close that the boy had already heard the news that Baylou was gone. His eyes were red and puffy from crying, but the tears on his face had already dried or been brushed away.

"I'm so sorry, Willie," said Luke with compassion. "I'm sure you're going to miss her. I know I will."

"Go away!" exploded Willie. "Ruined! All ruined, for what? Now what? Who will I have now?!"

"Yeah, I get that," replied Luke. "It was a rare thing you two had."

"Mum says Baylou was really old," Willie offered after several minutes of silence. "Doesn't make it better."

"No, I can see that it wouldn't, not right now anyway. But you may feel a bit differently about it in a few years. And when you're my age, you find you look back on people you've known who've really made a difference in your life and be mostly happy you had that time, instead of being mostly sad that they're gone."

"Mostly sad, for a long time," whispered Willie.

"Yeah, I know how that feels. But I wanted to let you know that I was with Baylou when she died. And the last thing she said to me, was to tell you goodbye. She said she knew you'd be OK."

"What?" he demanded, sitting up straight.

"She said, "'Tell Willie goodbye. Such a good boy, he'll be alright,'" replied Luke. "Those were her very last words."

Willie turned away then and Luke was glad the boy couldn't see the tears in his own eyes.

"Funeral next week, if you want to come," Willie called out, his back still turned.

"I'll be there," Luke replied. "And do you remember that pretty girl you saw me with at the meeting?"

"Tall one, pretty eyes?"

"Yeah, that's the one. Jenny's her name. It turns out she's Baylou's daughter that she had to give up for adoption years ago, at least we think that's what happened. Baylou named her Raven. Is it alright if I bring her to the funeral? I think she'd like to meet you."

"Sure," said Willie with a slight quiver in his voice as he brushed the tears from his eyes.

The boy then set his shoulders back and turned to face Luke.

"Me too," he added resolutely.

"Good. I'll see you then," said Luke firmly, then lifted his hand in a wave as he turned to leave.

Chapter 46

Monday 22 January 10 am

Jenny called Luke just as he was finishing his morning coffee.

"I've got some bad news," she began.

"Peg was showing signs of early labour this morning and called her doctor, who insisted she be air-lifted out to Victoria right away even though the contractions eventually stopped. Apparently, the doctor has been telling Peg for months that she shouldn't try to stay here for the birth, and that even before the earthquake the hospital wouldn't have been equipped to manage the long-term care of two premature infants if they came early. Since Ian's still in Victoria waiting to get *here*, she finally agreed to go. She's at the hospital now but they've arranged to fly her out as soon as the weather clears down south, which they think might be tomorrow or the next day.

"But that leaves just me and Pete to take care of all the animals. Which means I won't be able to see you much at all. I know we were planning to try and spend some time together this week but I really shouldn't leave, even for a few hours at a time."

"Why don't I come and help?" asked Luke, after a half-minute of thought. "I could use a break after all the drama of the last week or so, and it will give us even more time together."

"I'd like that," said Jenny shyly, suddenly forgetting her half-hearted resolve to let things cool down between them. What Luke proposed was definitely a ramping back up but it felt natural and comfortable.

"I can come out today, if that's not too soon for you," he said in the voice that made her heart melt.

"Even right now would not be too soon for me," she teased.

Luke packed a bag and left a note for Blake, who was still at work, probably busy helping to mop up the bureaucratic mess the wolves had left behind.

Jenny was out feeding the chickens when Luke pulled into the yard. After a perfunctory kiss, she put him to work feeding the surviving pig and mucking out her pen.

"The faster we get the farm chores done, the sooner you can help me in the kitchen with the baking," she called out to him cheerfully.

However, they never made it to the kitchen after the chores. Jenny was willingly distracted by Luke's amorous intensions after she showed him the bedroom they would occupy while he was there.

It was at least an hour before anything was happening in the kitchen and even then, Luke wasn't much help.

"You could measure some flour for me," Jenny had complained at one point, without much conviction.

"I'd much rather watch you," he'd replied with a smile. "I'm much better as an official taster anyway."

He had indeed just sat watching her as she made a batch of muffins and shaped the bread she'd started earlier in the day, and then put them all in the oven.

"You could at least get the milk out of fridge for tea," she said with fake exasperation, after the muffins were done.

As they sat munching their snack, Pete came in from the barn. Jenny introduced the men and Pete took a place at the table.

"Jenny tells me you're sure the wolves are gone," Pete said, facing Luke. "Is that the whole truth or just what you told her to make her feel safe? I really need to know, since I was really counting on Ian bringing some rifles home with him."

"Yes, as far as I know, any wolves that survived the hunt Uncle Jack organized are likely gone, probably moved east," Luke replied. "I'm going to guess, however, that there may be a slight threat to the remaining animals on the farm even from a few lone survivors, just because they'll remember there's vulnerable prey here. But I've brought my own rifle with me and I have my sidearm as well, so we're not without protection."

"You didn't tell me you had guns!" said Jenny with consternation.

"Did you think a Mountie went around without them, even if he was on leave?" asked Luke with a smile.

"I don't know, I guess I never really thought about it," she replied defensively. "It doesn't actually bother me, I'm just surprised, that's all."

"Let's not worry too much about it, alright?" said Luke, looking over at Pete. "But to be on the safe side, I'll hang out in the yard this afternoon and stand guard until after dark. And I'll get up before sunrise and watch over the animals until it gets full light. Those seem to have been your most vulnerable times in the past, so if we don't see any wolves over the next few days, I think we can probably say you're in the clear."

***

Later that afternoon, Luke walked around the yard keeping watch—rifle in hand—as Jenny locked the chickens up and Pete started rounding the Shetlands up to put into the barn. Just as he got the stocky ponies haltered up to lead them inside, the donkeys started to bray.

Luke ran over to the edge of barn just in time to see a lone black wolf slinking along the fence-line toward the ice cream shed, where the sole remaining goat stood perched on the roof.

Amid the cacophony of the screaming donkeys and the frightened horses, Luke took aim and fired. The wolf dropped immediately and Luke ran over to make sure he'd made a lethal shot.

"And here I thought I was going to get out of this crisis without ever seeing one of these wolves," he said in awe as Jenny and Pete ran over the join him. "Smaller than I expected."

"Rex Matterson—the wolf biologist I talked to a couple weeks ago—told me these sea wolves were smaller than usual but you wouldn't know that from the tracks I saw. These guys really must struggle to survive here on the coast."

"Still bloody efficient killers," Pete replied, pulling back the wolf's top lip. "Look at the size of its teeth!"

"Yeah, that's the truth," Luke replied. "This one must have some dog genes in it, maybe from an ancestor that bred with a dog decades ago. Rex told me that too—fully wild wolves aren't naturally black. I wonder if that's why it managed to survive the stress of living around here?"

"Does that really matter right now?" asked Jenny, her frustration apparent as she glanced over at Luke. "Aren't you missing the point? Is this one the last of them?"

"I hope so," he replied evenly. "I'll let Sergeant Hammond know we've dealt with this one, I really can't keep that from him. But I'll stand guard in the yard for the next few nights and mornings anyway, just to be on the safe side."

The farm animals finally settled down enough to be bedded down. After Luke's call, Sergeant Hammond sent Cole out to collect the wolf carcass. That's when Luke found out what he'd missed while he'd been gone.

Chapter 47

Monday 22 January 3 pm

While Luke was busy dealing with livestock management and the lone wolf attack at the Menagerie, some unpleasant business was underway at the RCMP detachment downtown.

"The Pritchards are on their way in," Sergeant Hammond said to Cole. "Parents of the two boys that died surfing at Wickaninnish. The father just called from the beach asking for directions into the office. Pull that stuff out of evidence for them, will you? Put it all in the interview room, including the boards."

"Sure, Sarge," replied Cole. "Do they know yet, about the other stuff?"

"No, just about the boards."

"Oh, boy, that'll be rough," commented Cole.

"Yeah, well, no way around it," Hammond replied. "I'll deal with it."

Hammond told the receptionist to send the Pritchards into his office when they arrived and then went there himself to think about what he would say to them.

He didn't have much time for reflection, however, as there was soon a knock on the door signalling the parents arrival.

265

After introductions and some perfunctory remarks, Hammond led them into the interview room, where a banker-style evidence box sat on a table. Two badly battered surf boards were propped up against the far wall.

Mrs. Pritchard burst into tears when she saw the boards and went over to touch them. Her husband gave her a minute and then went to join her.

"Why don't you both sit down," suggested Hammond, as gently as he could. "I know this situation is very hard but I have some other news about the deaths of your sons."

"What?" asked the father. "Whoever called to say they'd found the boards and the van said the boys were still classified as missing. Are you saying you now know for sure they're dead?"

"Yes, Mr. Pritchard, we think so," replied Hammond, causing Mrs. Pritchard to moan in anguish. "I'm sorry, I know we said before that the boys had probably drowned and the bodies swept out to sea. But we know now that that's likely not what happened. Due to other attacks by wolves around town over the last few weeks, we had to consider the possibility that your sons were attacked by wolves at some point during their time here. So, we had a team search the woods near the place where their van was found."

Hammond took the lid off the box at his elbow and reached in with one hand.

"The search team found some bits of torn wetsuit, a flare of the type also found in your son's van, and a dive watch," he said gently, pulling out a watch in a plastic evidence bag. "Can you tell me if this watch belonged to one of your boys?"

The father gingerly accepted the watch from Hammond and examined it closely as his wife looked on. When he nodded his head, she again burst out sobbing.

"We gave Jamie this for his last birthday," he said in a low voice. "He'd always wanted one, but they're really expensive, you know? But I could see he wasn't going to grow out of his passion for surfing, so we thought he'd be safer having one."

His voice cracked then and he turned for comfort from his wife.

Hammond gave them a few minutes and then cleared his throat.

"We still need confirmation from the coroner but we're sure now that your boys were also killed by wolves," he said. "I'm so sorry for your loss."

"Did you find the bodies?" asked Mrs. Pritchard, tears flowing down her face. "Where are their bodies?"

"I'm sorry, no, the watch is all we have," Hammond replied, with genuine compassion. "The bite marks on the watch strap are almost conclusive evidence, as are the bits of torn wetsuit, that they were attacked in predatory fashion. We'll probably be able to get DNA from them. Then we'll test to see if they match any other wolves we've identified in relation to other attacks we've had over the last few weeks."

"What does that mean?" she asked, shaking her head in confusion.

"I think he means the wolves ate them," said Mr. Pritchard gently, which caused his wife to moan even louder, her sorrow compounded.

"I'm so very sorry, I know it must be devastating to lose both of your sons this way," said Hammond soothingly.

The boys' father sat up straight then and dried his eyes with his sleeve.

"I've been reading the news reports about these attacks," he said, his voice now under control. "One of them claimed Parks Canada officials knew there'd been a significant escalation of very threatening encounters with wolves since before Christmas but didn't make that information public. Is that true?"

"I'm not sure about that, Mr. Pritchard," replied Hammond. "I've heard that rumour too. There hasn't been a full-fledged investigation yet. But I'm sure details like that will come out in the formal inquests that will be conducted for all the deaths that occurred, including the one for your sons."

"Well, I'll tell you this," said Pritchard, his voice now rising in anger. "If it turns out that weeks before my sons died, that they knew and didn't say—that Parks officials knew wolves were going after people, not just dogs, but wolves attacking people in a seriously threatening manner—they're going to have a massive lawsuit on their hands."

"And I'll tell you this," he added, his face turning red. "I'll sue those First Nations bands too, the ones insisting wolves are the victims here and needed to be protected."

"My *children* needed protection!" he wailed loudly. "Their pandering to vicious animals got my sons killed!"

Mr. Pritchard broke down then and his wife took him in her arms.

Hammond sat still for a few minutes and then stood.

"Again, I'm so sorry for your loss. Let's go back to my office and deal with the paperwork. All of these items will be kept as evidence for the inquest. The coroner's office will be in touch with you about that when the time comes, and I'm sorry, I don't know how long that will take."

Half an hour later, he watched them leave the detachment through the front doors. He shook his head at the tragedy they had suffered and the grief he knew was still on the horizon for them. There was no way around it.

He also knew there was bound to be major repercussions over the community's response to the wolf attacks. However, he was sure most of it wasn't going to land on what the Mounties had done—the biggest hammer was bound to be aimed squarely at Parks Canada officials.

Chapter 48

Monday 22 January 9 pm

They all ate without saying much after Cole departed. Pete returned to his own quarters immediately after he'd finished eating, turning down Luke's offer of an after-dinner whiskey.

Jenny and Luke took their drinks into the bedroom but only a few sips of the amber liquid were consumed before they got distracted by Luke lifting Jenny's sweater over her head.

"I have to be up early," he murmured into her ear as justification, although it was clear she wasn't expecting him to provide an excuse.

The next few mornings and late afternoons passed uneventfully, at least as far as predator visitations were concerned. Luke relaxed some of his vigilance and he and Jenny spent companionable days fixing fences, feeding chickens, and chopping fire wood while Pete looked after the horses and the donkeys.

By Friday afternoon, when it really seemed like the threat of another wolf attack was over, Luke disappeared into the barn for a private chat with Pete. He emerged an hour later with Big Ben hooked up to his little carriage, prepared to take Jenny on a ride out along the local trail.

Fortunately, the temperature had risen somewhat over the last few days and it hadn't rained for hours, providing almost idyllic conditions for a winter's day on the west coast.

"I never would have taken you for such a romantic," Jenny said tenderly, her hand on his thigh as Luke struggled to get the hang of driving the big draft horse.

"Only when it counts," he replied with a grin. "I expect big brownie points for trying, it's harder than it looks!"

Fortunately, Big Ben knew what was expected of him and settled into the hour-long ride. No wolves exploded out of the woods to spoil their journey and after their return, Jenny rewarded Luke with the attention he'd hoped for in the bedroom.

Luke's romantic bliss was shattered when he returned to his trailer on the pretext of picking up some clean clothes so he could return a call he'd missed from the division chief in Vancouver. From the little information the chief had provided in his message, he suspected it was a conversation he wouldn't want Jenny to overhear.

He was quite right.

That one phone call blew up his idyllic plan to make a home here in Tofino and a future with Jenny.

Chapter 49

Tuesday 30 January 11:00 pm

Bundled up against the cold, Luke and Jenny sat on the beach under the light of the full moon, where they'd retreated after Baylou's funeral.

It had been more like a memorial, really, rather than a funeral, which had been a short but emotionally-charged affair. There had been a heartfelt eulogy from Willie which he managed to accomplish with very few words, while Betsy spoke at more length. Luke had encouraged Jenny to say something but she insisted she hadn't really known Baylou at all and was an outsider amongst these friends of hers.

However, Willie clearly didn't feel the same way. He'd proudly introduced her around to his family as Baylou's daughter and they'd all embraced her warmly. Luke felt honoured to finally meet the boy's parents and grandparents.

Now, sitting with his arm around Jenny, he felt he finally had to share his news.

"I've been offered a job," he began with some trepidation.

"A photo shoot?" she replied without much interest, still looking out to sea.

"No. A police job," he replied, looking over at her.

"Here in Tofino?" she asked with a bit more interest. "That would be great, if that's what you want."

"No, not here. Back east. It's a different sort of gig than I've usually done."

That was putting it mildly.

Three days ago, he'd returned the call from the division chief in Vancouver, who'd somehow tracked him down after a series of inquiries had bounced from one end of the country to the other.

"Command want someone to go undercover on a new research vessel parked out on Hudson Bay—a retrofitted oil rig," the chief began. "The local detachment think they might have a murder on their hands but it's not something they can deal with. So far, there's only reports of suspicious behaviour and a missing researcher. They can't tell yet if it's a tragic accident, a polar bear attack, or foul play.

"I understand you've sent in your resignation but command has decided that if you want full retirement benefits, you'll have to take on one last job. This assignment is not normally how we deal with things but this is a unique situation. And when this request came through, it seemed like it might be a good fit for you. You've dealt with Arctic conditions. It's not a wildlife issue exactly—the researchers are there to study polar bears but the potential murder is strictly a police matter. And we've heard good things from the sergeant in charge out there in Tofino about how you've dealt with the wolf attack issue."

Luke's head was spinning with the news and what it meant for the decisions he'd been wrestling with over the last few weeks.

"You want me to go undercover, as a polar bear researcher?" he asked, trying to buy some time.

"Well, that's what's been proposed but I suppose it could be something else—I'm not sure anyone's thought it through completely yet," the chief replied.

"Could I bring someone with me?" Luke asked, thinking out loud.

"Why would you ask that?"

"I'm just thinking that perhaps if I went with a woman and we were posing as journalists, it might be more credible—and we might get the information we need quicker than if I went alone," he responded.

"I guess that could work, depending on who you're thinking of as a partner," the chief said. "Think about it, but we need a response quickly. End of the month at the latest."

Now, sitting under the stars with Jenny on the second-last day of the month, he tried to explain.

"I've asked Blake to come with me," he began gently. "She's been needing a break from small-town policing for a while now and I thought this job might be right up her alley. I don't think we'd be gone very long, perhaps a few weeks. And then I'd come back and get you."

"Get me?" asked Jenny, perplexed.

"Well, with Baylou gone I figured you probably didn't want to stay here. Blake and I are thinking maybe this job could be a kick-starter for the two of us setting up as private investigators. But those kind of jobs usually are big-city gigs, at least associated with bigger cities than Tofino. With your experience, it seemed to me you can probably work anywhere."

"But I *do* want to stay," Jenny whispered, just audible above the sound of the waves. "Peg needs me to stay at the farm until she and Ian get back and will need me even more once she comes home with the twins. And with the wolves gone, I kind of like it at the farm again. Willie needs me too, I think.

"He and his parents were calling me 'Raven' at the funeral tonight, introducing me around like I was suddenly part of the family. And I'd miss Betsy if I left, she's turned into a real friend. I didn't think I'd ever say these words out loud, but I really don't want to go, not ever. Even with Baylou gone, I still have roots here. This place feel more like home than anywhere I've ever lived."

It was Luke's turn to gaze out to sea, watching the swells advance relentlessly towards him until they crashed onto the shore at his feet.

"I don't want to leave you, Jenny," he said ruefully. "I didn't think I'd ever again feel so strongly about anyone after I lost Kate. It's not just that I need this Hudson Bay job to secure my pension—although that's part of it—but I'm too young to just retire and do nothing productive.

I've got another 20 or 30 years to do meaningful work. I can see now that the photography thing isn't really a long-term solution for me. I need to see if doing private investigations could fit the bill."

"It might not be any better than the photography," Jenny pointed out.

"That's true but I won't know unless I try," he replied, giving her shoulder a squeeze. "But I'm not going to say goodbye just yet. I'll come back after we've got this job done, when I know for sure."

"I'll hold you to that, but I'm really going to miss you," said Jenny tearfully. "I'm grateful we've had this time. I don't know what I'd have done if you hadn't been here."

"Don't get all melodramatic on me," teased Luke. "You'll be fine. I should be back before Peg and the babies come home, you'll hardly notice I'm gone."

"Oh, I'll notice," Jenny whispered, sitting up straighter and working harder to fight back the tears. "Suddenly having a bed all to myself will be hard to ignore, given how much space you take up."

Luke laughed out loud and stood up, reaching down to take Jenny's hand. He pulled her up to stand beside him and turned to take her in his arms. His bear hug turned seamlessly into a deep kiss, both hands holding her beautiful face.

When they came up for air, he wiped a few of her lingering tears away with his thumb.

"Night's not over yet," he whispered in her ear.

Taking her hand, he lead her up the beach to his truck and then to his bed.

Epilogue

Wednesday 31 January 9:00 am

Luke had just returned from driving Jenny home after a night with not much sleep when his phone rang. The display indicated the RCMP division chief was calling for his answer.

"Your proposal has been approved," said the chief. "You and Palmer will go undercover at the Hudson 57 research station on Hudson Bay, reporting to the Churchill detachment until the situation is resolved, after which your employment will be terminated with full pension. If Palmer stays on, she will be re-assigned, but we can't guarantee where she'll be placed. She'll have to take her chances, as always."

"We'll use priority status to make sure we're out on the next plane to Vancouver this afternoon," Luke replied. "If you can get us connecting flights to Winnipeg and Churchill, we should be able to touch down sometime tomorrow, pending weather delays."

"Excellent," said the chief. "I'll let Churchill know to expect you. They'll arrange transport to the research station and pave your cover story. Officially, you'll be free-lancers writing a big feature for the Daily Chronicle, a London-based UK newspaper. Paperwork for both of you, including plane tickets, will be sent immediately to the Tofino office."

As he disconnected, he saw Blake exiting her trailer and stepped outside to wave her over.

"It's all set," he shouted across the deck. "Put your raingear under the bed and dig out your parka. We're going to the Arctic."

"I hope like hell we're doing the right thing," she replied, shaking her head as she closed the gap between them.

"You and me both," said Luke with a grin, handing her a cup of coffee.

"I think I may actually miss Cooper," said Blake wistfully.

"Jenny said Peg was very happy to let him be the farm cat at the Menagerie," Luke replied matter-of-factly. "He didn't seem at all concerned when I dropped him off with her this morning. I think he'll fit right in."

"And did you finalize the deal with the barge? It makes me nervous to leave before that's taken care of."

"Relax," said Luke, laying his hand on her arm. "Our landlord John has it all arranged. He's hired drivers to take both of our trucks and trailers down to the dock in three weeks and get them loaded onto the barge for transport to Vancouver. It was the earliest date he could get. The city has hired the barge to bring in fuel and food without charge but the scaled reservation fees they've imposed for space outbound means we have to compete with logging trucks and tourists with huge recreation vehicles. In other words, it'll cost us. But the good news is there's space at the Vancouver detachment impound lot for both rigs to sit for free until we can get back for them."

"And then what?" asked Blake, eyebrows raised.

"Right now, I haven't got a clue," Luke responded. "We'll have to figure that out as we go along. But at least we'll both have a place to sleep, no matter where we end up. You were certainly right about that."

He raised his coffee cup in salute to hers.

"To Hudson Bay!" they chimed in restrained unison, some of the implied cheeriness clearly lacking.

"What the hell have we gotten ourselves into, partner?" muttered Blake, shaking her head.

Luke just shrugged at her and grinned.

About The Author

 Susan Crockford is a professional zoologist with a penchant for storytelling. She has a special interest in the evolution of wild wolf to domestic dog and has written a 2004 Ph.D. dissertation on the topic and contributed to a 2025 paper in *Science* magazine (Issue 6774).

DON'T RUN is Susan's third novel for readers who prefer their science 'lite' and love a good story. Her first novel was EATEN, a polar bear attack thriller set in Newfoundland, followed by UPHEAVAL, the story of a sea ice tsunami that hits Cape Breton Island, Nova Scotia.

Her book website is at www.susancrockford.com. She writes online at www.susancrockford.substack.com ("Biology Bites") and www.polarbearscience.com.

You can find all of her books on Amazon.

www.ingramcontent.com/pod-product-compliance
Lightning Source LLC
Chambersburg PA
CBHW060407260626
47160CB00006B/2467